Mary Scott lives in Devon where she teaches creative writing. Her first book, *Nudists May be Encountered*, a collection of stories, was published by Serpent's Tail in 1991

Praise for *Nudists May be Encountered*
'Each story forms an exquisitely executed comment on male female relationships, observed with a wit and observation that mark the debut of a fine talent.'
Time Out

'Scott's tales are elegant, observant and smart, with serious mania, misery and experimentation lurking just beneath.'
City Limits

'Ironic, funny, panicky. The title is fair warning: some odd private parts are on display.'
The Face

'Scott is always on the lookout for something smart to do, whether in use of language, plot or characters.'
The Canberra Times

'Tales of distinctive wit and sharp social comment.'
The Sunday Times

Other 90s titles

Keverne Barrett
Unsuitable Arrangements

Neil Bartlett
Ready to Catch Him Should He Fall

Suzannah Dunn
Darker Days Than Usual

James Lansbury
Korzeniowski

Silvia Sanza
Alex Wants to Call it Love

Susan Schmidt
Winging It

Mary Scott
Nudists May Be Encountered

Atima Srivastava
Transmission

Lynne Tillman
Absence Makes the Heart

Colm Tóibín
The South
(Winner of the 1991 *Irish Times* Aer Lingus Fiction Prize)

Margaret Wilkinson
Ocean Avenue

....

not in newbury

....

Mary Scott

This volume was published with assistance from the
Ralph Lewis Award at the University of Sussex.

Acknowledgement: To the Arts Council of Great Britain 1992

Library of Congress Catalog Card Number: 92–60140

British Library Cataloguing-in-Publication Data
Scott, Mary
   Not in Newbury
   I. Title
   823.914[F]

   ISBN 1-85242-271-8

First published 1992 by
Serpent's Tail, 4 Blackstock Mews, London N4
and 401 West Broadway #2, New York, NY 10012

Set in 10½/14pt Goudy by Contour Typesetters, Southall, London
Printed in Great Britain by Cox & Wyman Ltd,
of Reading, Berkshire

not in newbury

it takes a thief

Alice was trying to wriggle through a crowd of people to the drinks table when her way was barred by a broad, green-sweatered back. 'Excuse me,' she said. 'If I could just squeeze past . . .' but the back turned and became a front and a voice above her head which asked, 'Red or white? I can reach.' 'White please,' Alice replied and studied the owner of the back as he stretched one arm over people's shoulders, picked up a full glass and handed it to her.

'Thanks,' said Alice. 'I'm sure I should know you. Are you a buyer?'

'No,' said the man. 'I'm a wordsmith.'

'Why are you wearing Doc Martens with red shorts?' Alice couldn't resist asking. 'And what sort of pieces do you make?'

'All these people,' he gestured dismissively at the crowd, 'expect a wordsmith to look eccentric. I'm a Brutalist. My work's on show all over. You'll know exactly who I am as soon as I tell you my name.'

He told her. 'Oh, that's who you are,' she exclaimed. Later he came home with her.

Alice had never had an affair with a fellow wordsmith before: and certainly not with one who was the darling of the critics in the way Peter was. 'I can introduce you to all the right people,' he promised. 'People who'll make a real difference to your career.' He finished lacing his boots, looked at her and frowned. 'But you ought to do something about your image. It doesn't help to go around looking like a bimbo.'

Alice had just pulled a pink micro-minidress down over her behind and was admiring herself in the mirror. 'I thought this looked nice.'

'Not for the sort of people you'll be rubbing shoulders with tonight. If you want them to take you seriously.'

'What should I wear then?' She inspected Peter's heavy boots, his white jogging pants and his flak jacket. 'I don't have anything like your stuff.'

He strode across the room and flung open the wardrobe door. 'Use your imagination,' he instructed, then sat down on the bed to watch her try things on. Finally, when she put on a pair of red-and-yellow tartan trews with white trainers, a skimpy black lycra top and a black straw hat bought for Sue and Lawrence's wedding, he declared she was ready.

Off they went to another party where Alice met all the right people; she and Peter were even photographed as they left by a couple of the lesser paparazzi. 'Well,' thought Alice as she snuggled down that night, 'I suppose I could consider I've really arrived.'

Certainly she had come a long way since she first started building a word wall back in school.

In public Alice's affair with Peter was gratifying; in private it was exquisite. The two of them poured uncut words over each other like torrents of glittering gems. Alice poured more torrents than Peter did because her productivity was, as ever, high. But, as Peter spent a year on average in crafting a single piece, his torrent was less of a torrent, more of a trickle. As time went on the trickle grew thinner and thinner until one day, after he had been staying at Alice's flat for several months, it dried up entirely. He spent the whole day staring gloomily at a big, black chunk of unhewn word-ore while Alice sat beside him churning out jewel after sparkling jewel. She stopped work and offered him a cup of tea. He shook his head and glared at her. 'The trouble with your pieces,' he informed her, 'is that they have no soul. Just because they sell, doesn't make them art.'

All the same, that night when Alice was asleep, Peter packed up all her best words and all her half-finished word jewels and made off with them, not even leaving a note to say goodbye.

In the weeks that followed she heard nothing of him, except what she read in the papers; she read that he was doing well. Of course he wasn't foolish enough to try to sell any of Alice's pieces, but it was clear where the inspiration for his new work lay. She didn't have a leg to stand on though; there was no copyright on ideas.

If only I had been more careful,' Alice moaned to herself and to anyone else who would listen (Sue mainly). 'If only I'd thought twice. It's all my own fault.' At this point she invariably burst into tears. 'I should have known better, me of all people,' she wailed between sobs. 'When you look at what happened to my word wall.'

'That was ages ago,' Sue protested. 'You'd forgotten all about it till now.' She took a look at Alice's mutinous face and added hastily, 'Though I do remember you were inconsolable for days.'

It was quite true that Alice had scarcely given her word wall even a passing thought for years; the way her career had taken off it was water under the bridge. But now, what had happened way back when, seemed a fresh and intolerable grievance.

∗

It was a bright, chilly March morning, the sort of morning on which most children long to be out and running around shrieking; but not Alice. When she arrived at school she handed Miss Burrows a note. The note, she knew, explained that Alice had a cold and should stay in at break. The note was signed with Alice's mother's name. Alice had made up the note and forged the signature.

But even in those days, Alice had a way with words. Miss Burrows accepted the note without question and in due course Alice sat and smugly watched the other children falling over their feet in their rush to reach the playground. She waited for Miss Burrows to follow, then took a handful of words out of her satchel and carried on building her wall.

Alice's word wall was going to be the biggest word wall in the world. Perhaps it was going to be the only word wall; she had never heard of anyone else building one — but then there were lots of things she had never heard of, Alice knew. In particular, there were lots of words.

She smoothed out several of the folded up pieces of paper in front of her. 'Renegade', she read on one. She had found it the afternoon before in a Western novel in the library. She looked it up in her *Collins English Gem Dictionary*: 'deserter, apostate,' she read. What was an apostate? She turned to the 'a's; apostasy meant 'abandonment of one's religion or other faith.' She was sure 'renegade' had not meant quite that in the Western; but she stuck it on the word wall anyway.

The classroom door banged. Was it one of the boys? If it was reedy Richard she'd be all right. But suppose it wasn't? Alice pulled the word wall hastily round her. 'Hello, what have we here?' said a voice. Bert Langley's voice.

'What's Alice doing in here by herself do you reckon, Greg?'

Bert went on; which meant Greg Wale was with him. Alice trembled.

'Hey, Alice, what's that mess of paper?' Greg sniggered and turned to Bert. 'Shall we set fire to it? I've got some matches.'

Bert laughed. 'I've a better idea,' he announced. 'You know that project Miss Burrows says we have to do?' Greg nodded. 'Let's take this whatever-it-is and say it's ours. As Alice made it, it's bound to get good marks.' He stepped forward.

Alice grabbed a couple of words and hurled them as hard as she could at the two grinning faces in front of her. But they didn't make any difference; the boys took the wall, Miss Burrows gave them a gold star each for it and Alice had to start again from scratch.

She continued building her wall on and off for years, but she never finished it; it was such a big project. By the time she started college, where she enrolled for a course in wordsmith-ship, she had forgotten all about it; besides her tutors said her talents lay in producing much smaller, rather exquisite items.

It seemed they were right; even before she received her City and Guilds she made something of a name for herself as a designer of tiny, glittering word jewels. What was more, there turned to be quite a market for them.

After college Alice shared a rented flat with Sue. They'd kept in touch since primary school and now they had a great time arguing — especially about Sue's boyfriend Lawrence's politics (he was a Trotskyist, although otherwise Alice rather liked him).

Alice had long since supplemented her *Collins English Gem* with a *Penguin English Dictionary* and a *Roget's Thesaurus*. Now she decided to develop convictions; she bought a copy of the

Feminist Dictionary. Some of her designs during this period were considered by (mainly male) critics to be 'less accessible . . . more political statements than, strictly speaking, works of art . . .' But they still sold well.

Alice could afford to buy a flat. She found the ideal place — in North London, just inside the 071 telephone area. She loved the flat but dreaded breaking the news to Sue. When she did, Sue gave a sigh of relief and said, 'That's terrific. Lawrence and I didn't know how to tell you, but we want to move in together.'

Alice had a locksmith install a mortice on each of the doors and locks on the windows of the flat. Then she bought a Moulinex food processor, a Hotpoint washer/dryer, an Amstrad PCW and several black, high-tech bookshelves. She also bought a *Dictionary of Euphemisms and Obscenities* and began to design erotic word jewels which sold even better.

By now Alice was an up and coming member of the London wordsmiths' scene. She was invited to lots of wordsmiths' parties — and at one of the parties she met Peter.

In the months after Peter left, Alice didn't wear the red-and-yellow tartan trews again. Nor did she wear micro-minidresses. She draped herself in a long, black tunic over tight black leggings and dragged her hair off her face in a black band. She stopped going to parties. She stopped eating and grew thin.

Both Sue and Lawrence (who now voted Labour so Alice liked him even more) tried to make light of the catastrophe. 'It happens to all of us at one time or another,' Sue assured her. 'Some men are like that.' 'You must expect at least a couple of burglaries every twenty years if you live in the 071 area,' Lawrence informed her. 'That's why our insurance premiums are so high.' But Alice murmured sadly, 'It never happened to me before,' and 'Insurance money won't bring back my words.'

Worst of all, Alice produced no more word jewels. 'Because I can't,' she said when Sue came round for the umpteenth time to cheer her up. 'Because I daren't.'

'Why don't you dare?' asked Sue. 'Explain.'

'You won't understand,' wailed Alice. 'You're not a word-smith, so how could you?'

'Try me,' said Sue, then held up her hand before Alice could speak. 'No, on second thoughts, wait. I've brought a bottle of gin. A couple of glasses of that should help to get it off your chest.'

'There isn't any ice in the fridge,' complained Alice as though this were not her fault. 'The glasses are all dirty; and there's no tonic. So we can't.'

'No such word as can't,' said Sue firmly. Alice muttered, 'You've no right to say that. You don't know anything about words,' but Sue went on: 'We'll drink it warm. You do a spot of washing up and I'll nip out to the off-licence.'

When she returned she found Alice hadn't moved an inch; she was still sitting on the fitted carpet in the middle of the living room with her arms clasped round her knees and her head bowed. 'The picture of dejection,' said Sue sarcastically. 'Pull yourself together and pull up a pew.' Alice rose and dumped herself in one of her upright chairs. Sue went into the kitchen, washed and dried two glasses, carried them into the living room, poured a large measure of gin and a smaller one of tonic into each of them, handed Alice her drink and sat opposite her at the table. 'Now,' she said. 'I'm all ears. Spit it out.'

'Well,' said Alice, then paused, took a gulp of gin and spluttered, 'Good Lord, you've made this strong,' took another gulp and continued, 'You see it's not like he was any ordinary man or any ordinary burglar,' and stopped. Sue picked up the gin bottle, refilled Alice's glass and waited.

'If he'd stolen anything else — the Moulinex or the Hotpoint, say,' Alice went on, 'it wouldn't have been so bad. Or if he'd been an ordinary burglar or even an ordinary lover and he'd stolen the words. But he was a wordsmith and he knew what the words meant to me.' Alice gave a small belch. 'Also I thought I'd really made it when he and I got together. He was so respectable.'

'Respectable?' Sue raised her eyebrows. 'In those extra-ordinary clothes?'

'That is respectable for a wordsmith. He said so.' Alice sniffed twice. 'I can't trust anyone any more,' she moaned. 'I don't know what to do.'

'Have some more of this.' Sue topped up her glass. 'And keep talking.'

'There's another thing,' Alice paused. 'You know what Lawrence said about burglaries in inner London?' Sue nodded. 'Well, he wasn't even a proper burglar. A burglar . . .' Alice took another mouthful of gin, 'is someone who breaks in from the outside not someone who is already in who takes things out.'

'Who says?' Sue helped herself to extra tonic.

'The *Collins English Gem*. "Burglary: noun. Forcible entry into a house after dark with intent to steal." I checked.'

'That's way out of date,' said Sue. 'You've had that dictionary since primary school. Nowadays a man can just as well be a burglar if you've let him in of your own accord. Think of those conmen who pretend to be from the Council and make off with pensioners' savings? And you must have read the statistics: most crimes against women are committed by men they know fairly well. Violent crimes usually, especially rape — there wasn't an element of that in your relationship, was there?'

'Rape,' said Alice bitterly. 'Verb transitive: assault sexually. Rape: noun: violent destruction or plundering. Rape: a conscious form of intimidation by which all men keep all women in a state of fear. From the *Collins English Gem*, the *Penguin English Dictionary* and the *Feminist Dictionary* in that order. It isn't in the *Dictionary of Euphemisms*.'

Sue leant her elbows on the table. 'Alice, let's get this straight. What you're suffering is not unusual.' She saw Alice was about to protest and said quickly, 'No, stop. I don't mean it feels any better for that. But there are organisations that can help. I've found the number of your local victim support scheme. They'll provide counselling. There's also the community police people who can advise on security in future. And you can phone the Rape Crisis Centre.'

'He didn't actually rape me,' admitted Alice. 'Not in the sense of the word which the Rape Crisis Centre would accept. Though,' she brightened, 'he did insist sometimes when I wasn't too keen.'

'Exactly.' Sue dumped her glass on the table and rose to her feet. 'I'm going now. I'm going to leave you the bottle as long as you promise me you'll go to bed. Have a good night's sleep. And first thing in the morning, call these numbers. I've written them all on the one sheet of paper.'

Alice slept on the living room floor with the half-empty bottle of gin beside her. In the morning she didn't phone any of the numbers Sue had left. Instead she put the top on the gin bottle and put the bottle in a plastic carrier bag; she gathered together the few words that Peter had left behind and put them in plastic bags too. She washed and dressed, took the bags and let herself out of the flat. She felt safer outside.

After that Alice became a . . . well . . . a bag lady. But instead of her bags being stuffed with old jumpers and jars of fish paste and bottles of gin (she soon drank the rest of what Sue'd brought), they were full of words: adverbs and adjectives, nouns, both proper and collective, verbs, both transitive and intransitive, prepositions, participles, gerunds, subjunctives and the odd expletive. Oh yes, Alice still collected words and she felt a lot better now she kept them all about her person.

But she collected so many she couldn't carry them all. From time to time when the words became too heavy or when one of the bags looked fit to burst, she went back to the flat, listened to the anxious enquiries from Sue on her answerphone, picked up her royalty cheques, stashed her bagfuls of words under the mattress and went out in search of new words. After a year or so Sue stopped leaving messages, the royalty cheques began to dry up and both the bedroom and the living room were piled high with bags of old words. Alice worried about leaving them in the flat but there was nothing she could do about it, and she always carried her best words with her.

One night, late, Alice was sitting with the other bag people under the South Bank Centre. Most other people had a cardboard box to sleep in; Alice had only her words. She arranged one bag as a pillow and settled the others on either side of her as insulation. But it was a cold night and she had nothing to cover her. She shivered.

'Excuse me,' said a man's voice. Alice shot bolt upright and gathered her words round her. 'Sorry, I didn't mean to make you jump,' the voice went on, 'I thought you might like my spare blanket.'

Alice looked at the blanket, then looked at the man who was holding it. He was dark — she could just see that — and seemed to be wearing a three-piece suit. 'Don't you dare touch my words,' she spat at him, but he replied, very mildly, 'Lady, I was only offering you a blanket.'

Alice took the blanket. It was good quality by the feel of it and very warm. She draped it over herself and her bags, pulling it right up to her chin. 'Most people don't have a spare blanket,' she said.

'It's knock-off,' said the man and turned away.

In the morning Alice woke to find herself wrapped in a pink fleecy blanket trimmed with pink satin ribbon. Beside her, wrapped in a similar blanket, lay the man in the suit. His head rested on a pillow bordered with pink lace. At the other end of the blanket, his feet in shiny black shoes poked out. Alice laughed and the man woke up.

'What's the joke?' he demanded.

'Sorry,' said Alice, 'is the pillow knock-off too?'

The man rolled over and rubbed his eyes: 'What if it is?'

'No problem,' said Alice, 'no hassle. It was the word I liked, the word "knock-off". I expect you want your blanket back.'

'No.' He sat up and fingered his unshaven chin. 'Plenty more where that came from. Not that I know where to put them.'

'Why not?' asked Alice. She noticed that his movement had shifted his blanket to reveal a small stack of videotapes beside his left arm.

'I've lost my lock-up garage,' said the man. 'The Council changed its policy. It would have been all right if I had somewhere to stay; but this woman I was living with threw me out because she didn't like having the knock-off in her place.

She even changed the locks.' He shook his head as though he couldn't believe it. 'I'm a thief, you see.'

'You mean you steal things?' Alice clutched at her bags of words.

'Got it in one.'

'What sort of things?'

'Videos, blanket sets, stereos, radios, portable TVs, CD players.'

'What about words? what about word jewels?'

'No good. It's a specialist market so you can't shift them quickly enough. And they're too easy to trace to the original owner.'

Alice let out a sigh of relief. 'I've enough money for two cups of tea,' she announced. 'If you'd like one, that is. In return for the loan of the blanket.'

The man nodded. Alice rose and folded her blanket neatly, but he said to leave it, he had nowhere to keep it. He left the videotapes too. Alice picked up all her bags. There were lots of bags, but he didn't offer to help.

The two of them walked up and down until they found a café. They went in. The café was very hot and very crowded. Alice had to put her bags under the table and she and the man sat with their feet on them. 'Two teas,' Alice said to the waitress. White, chipped, steaming mugs arrived and she and the man cupped their hands around them.

It was some time before either of them spoke. Then, 'You didn't help me carry my bags,' said Alice.

'Why should I?' The man raised his head from his mug and looked at her.

'I meant I liked that.' Alice smiled. 'You let me carry my own stuff.'

'Why shouldn't I? It's nothing to do with me.'

'I had bad experiences in the past with people running off with things,' Alice explained.

'That's nothing to do with me either.'

Alice thought for a moment, then asked, 'Where are you going afterwards?'

'Around. Out and about. Have to get some money from somewhere.' He rose to his feet. 'If the blankets are still there you're welcome to them. I'll see you.'

'Wait,' said Alice. She fumbled under the table. 'Would you like one of my words?' she asked, smiling as seductively as she knew how. She opened a bag to look for a nice, green juicy word to tempt him. She selected one, rubbed it on her sleeve and held it out to him on the flat of her hand as though offering it to a horse. 'It's a good one,' she assured him. 'In the old days I could have polished it up in no time — and sold it too. You could do that if you wanted.'

'No, thank you,' replied the man. 'I told you. It's a specialist market.' So Alice said, 'Would you like to come and see my flat?'

'What flat? You got a council place?'

Alice shook her head. 'I own it. Are you coming?' He nodded.

They arrived to find Alice's flat an utter tip. The sink was full of unwashed words from her last visit; the loo was clogged with Andrex with words all over it; and she and the man could hardly squeeze into the living room, it was so packed with bags of words. But they managed somehow and settled on the floor. Alice even found a bottle of apricot brandy in the kitchen and poured them a glass each.

'Tell me.' Alice paused and thought, 'tell me, where do you get your knock-off from?'

'I'm a thief. I thieve it.'

'Yes, but where from exactly?'

'Houses mainly. You have to pick your area. Highgate's a pretty decent patch. Hampstead's not bad either.'

'Oh good.' Alice grinned. 'They're both within walking distance. You can move in here. With a thief on the premises no one will dare steal my words. And you'll be able to pop up to Highgate and back of an evening.'

'Afternoon,' he corrected. 'I only thieve in the afternoons when people are out. Round about three o'clock, usually. If you do it in the evening it puts the wind up people; it makes for aggro; and besides you can't see what you're nicking in the dark.'

'How about it then?' Alice poured more brandy.

'It's not a bad idea,' he said slowly. He looked around the bag-filled room. 'One small hitch. There isn't enough space for you to live here, let alone me. Not with all this stuff.'

'Oh, that's no problem. The bags are only full of words. Now you're here I'll take them all out and put them all in a dictionary where they belong. It will take me years,' she smiled happily. 'But that won't matter because we can live on the money you make from stealing; and once I've cleared out all the words you'll be able to store your stuff in the flat until you sell it. It'll be perfect.'

And so it was. Every morning Alice emptied one of her bags and gave the bag to the man (whose name was Mike). Mike filled the bag with stolen goods, went out, sold them, bought food and returned to the flat for a late lunch. In the afternoon he went to Highgate to do his stealing. And in the meantime Alice put her words into a dictionary of her own; which was a much bigger project than building a word wall.

a clumsy effort at flight

The whoosh, the flutter, the sneeze, the hiccough, the chortle and the volcano — these were some of the names Alice had for different sorts of orgasm. They were private names, of course. Somewhere in the universe, she supposed, there might be a race whose people spent so much time at erotic pursuits that their language would have a separate word for all of these and for many more besides; like the Eskimos and their dozens of different terms for snow. In the meantime it was a shame that a single (and rather ugly-sounding) word had to cover for such a range of sensations: rather as if the term 'vegetable' was always made to stand for every taste, from that of the woodiest of carrots to the most succulent of mange-tout peas.

She sighed and settled her sunglasses on her nose. It was the glasses which had triggered off this train of thought — the Ray-Ban's she had found yesterday evening and which she hadn't set eyes on for ages: not since the sun last shone from London's skies in the autumn of the previous year.

Yesterday evening, she and Mike were in the middle of sex when he stopped and suggested, 'How d'you reckon this'd look through sunglasses?'

Alice didn't know and she hadn't the least idea where any sunglasses were. She tried the drawers of the bedside table, then the top shelf of the wardrobe, then under the bed. No joy. She tried the bathroom cabinet. She tried the fitted kitchen cupboards. Eventually she lit upon the (very dusty) Ray-Ban's behind a stack of bills on the living room mantelpiece and Mike found a cheap, blue-framed wraparound effort stuffed between a Thomas Hardy and a Joseph Heller on the bookshelves.

Alice went into the bathroom and wiped the Ray-Ban's with a sponge. She shivered. She was wearing nothing, the search had taken some time, it was still only early May and the evening was chilly. She returned to the bedroom, handed the Ray-Ban's to Mike, put on the wraparound and began again. But nothing looked different, it just looked darker.

'Actually,' said Alice. She removed the glasses. 'I'm not sure women care about how it looks. That is, I'm not sure I do.'

'No? Why not?'

'Don't know. Maybe I haven't thought about it.' Or maybe she didn't have the words.

This afternoon she stretched in the warmth of the bright May sun and tipped her face up to look — through the Ray-Ban's at the blue London sky. So much sky with so little — barring a wispy cloud or two — happening in it, yet so much happening in the city spread out below. Even in the sanctuary of her garden she could hear things happening. The woman at the back was shouting at her kids to stop the dog barking; violent crashings in the undergrowth next door indicated that the neighbours were having one of their periodic onslaughts on the garden; the hesitant playing of a recorder clashed with the lilt of Irish music from the pub at the end of the road; a siren wailed; and a window creaked which meant that the elderly guy three doors down was peering at her again. Good old London: where practically everything she did was shared — even if in some vicarious form — with a whole load of strangers.

The back door banged. Mike appeared. 'You staying out there much longer?' he demanded.

'Planning to. Why?'

'Isn't it coming on to rain?'

She inspected the sky again. Surprisingly, it was now full of clouds. A speck of moisture fell on her cheek. 'Expect it'll blow over,' she said hopefully. 'It's just a drop. Blowing wet as they say in the West Country.' She paused. 'Mike, do you realise how many phrases there are in English for it almost, but not quite, raining? Clouding over. Misting. Only a shower. There aren't nearly as many for when it actually starts doing it.'

Like sex.

'Pissing with rain. Chucking it down. Raining cats and dogs. Weather for ducks.' He smirked triumphantly. . . 'You're going to get soaked any minute,' and retreated indoors. Alice hurriedly picked up cushion and book and scurried from the downpour.

She dumped her cushion inside the back door and wandered into the living room. Mike was in the armchair watching racing on the TV, his feet on the coffee table between Alice's new cactus and a *Daily Mirror*. She went over to the window and watched the rain. The sky was a solid ceiling of low, grey clouds; the rain fell in sheets. 'It's set in for the day,' she informed him. He nodded up at her: 'Not in Newbury,' and turned back to the screen.

She wandered back to the sofa, sat with her feet curled under her and opened her damp book. She was reading *Bleak House* for the umpteenth time. She gazed at the print with unseeing eyes. Those words for orgasms. Why did she need them? It wasn't, she considered, that she wanted to use them in idle conversation. She didn't want to confide to one of the neighbours, 'Only a flutter yesterday,' or remark with a cheery thumbs up, 'Volcano again!' Nor did she want to keep Mike posted as to what level on the sexual Richter scale she reached. So what was it? She sunk her eyes to *Bleak House* then raised them again. It was — wasn't it — that there was something shifty, something missing about an experience which had no recognised name, which no one had considered worthy of naming. It meant that other people didn't rate it or maybe — the notion struck her like the sheet of water that drove against the windowpane — it meant other people didn't have it? A small step from there to the conviction that she was making it up.

She looked at Mike. He was slumped in his usual fashion in the chair, his legs sprawled apart, his chin sunk on his chest, his eyes fixed on the screen.

'Mike,' she said. 'Do you think we need to talk sometimes?'

'What about?'

'Oh, things.'

'No.'

'Why not?'

'Because I'm watching the racing.'

'You like watching things, don't you?' asked Alice.

'Sure.' He turned to look at her. 'Any reason why we don't go to bed?'

She shook her head.

In the bedroom: 'What would you like to do first?' he invited her to consider.

'Don't know. I'll have to think.' But the problem was a dearth of words. There were obscenities. Either that or the stuff of Mills & Boon. Or instructions.

She issued a few of those.

Mike liked watching. He liked to peer at things, a little frown of concentration creasing his brow. What was he watching? What was there to see? What, for instance, did an orgasm look like? She knew what his looked like, of course. But hers?

In the distance the dog barked and the squeaky recorder started up again, hesitantly. Alice could hear the neighbours attacking their garden once more, so it must have stopped raining.

Whoosh. Flutter. Sneeze.

'Hey.' Mike sat up sharply. 'Hey, did you see that?' he demanded, pointing. 'What?' asked Alice. She sat up too and discovered three little pink creatures fluttering on the floor. They were delicate and very pretty, like paper flowers. 'My God,' thought Alice, 'they look like off-cuts from one of Barbara Cartland's dresses.'

'There goes another one,' said Mike. It was skeetering across the bed. 'Oh dear,' said Alice.

'And another.' He brushed it gently off the sheet.

The ones on the floor were pattering about on soft, pink, dimpled toes, sneezing and whooshing and chortling. Several others scampered across the pillow and tumbled onto the carpet to join their fellows.

Mike climbed off the bed and stood looking at them all. They were running over his feet. 'I don't know what to say,' he said.

He was ankle deep in them. They flurried up from the floor, drifted and sank again like petals. Some of them began a clumsy effort at flight.

'Oh dear,' said Alice again. 'How embarrassing. I'd no idea they'd be so . . .'

'So what?'

'Well . . .' she stopped and thought. 'So . . . well . . . so frilly. So coy looking. So cutesey. So kitsch. Like something out of a suburban boudoir. Aren't they awful?'

Mike considered. He shook his head 'I think they look okay.' he nodded slowly. 'Yeah, they look okay.'

Alice frowned; then shrugged. 'I suppose it's you that has to look at them,' she admitted. 'So I guess that's all right?'

'Yeah. Except there are rather a lot.' He stirred a batch gently with one foot. 'What shall we do with them all?'

'I don't know.'

'I could open the window.'

'Okay.' She sat and clasped her hands around her knees as he opened it as far as the window lock would allow. The orgasms fluttered softly out into the garden. Alice rose and joined Mike at the window. Side by side they watched the delicate pink cloud float across the garden in the watery May sun, then over the garden walls into the neighbours' gardens and — possibly — through the neighbours' open windows, to settle one by one, like the petals of a rose on kitchen tables or on the pillow of a bed.

the tower room

There was a house in Alice's dreams, a house with many rooms. Sometimes, in the house, in the dreams, the rooms were arranged in a long line, leading one into another, so perhaps the house had been converted from a row of miners' or agricultural workers' cottages. Other times the house was a haphazard cluster of tall, tipsy chimneys above grey stone gables and walls, was a grange: not moated but towered. Yet again, it was crooked and Elizabethan with bulging, pargeted walls and secret rooms concealed during the eighteenth century to avoid window-tax and discoverable only after much tapping on interior walls and studying of exterior plans. This house — when the house was this house — fronted extensive farm buildings with cobbled yards; cool, cloistered walkways; and warm, clean barns smelling of sweet hay and horses, rustling with the movements of animals and the creak of leather.

But whichever house it was, there was always furniture to be arranged. In each dream the furniture came with the house, but with no instructions as to how it should be disposed, which room it would suit, against which wall or under which window it would best be placed. Those decisions were left to Alice.

She would work on the house — the houses — one room at a time, pushing and pulling at tables, 'walking' mahogany side-boards and heavy pine dressers across the carpet, sliding wing chairs into spots warmly lit by afternoon sun or by table lamps, arranging a coffee table at an angle to the open fire, filling a huge beaten copper jug with yellowed oak leaves and translucent pods of honesty and, finally, rubbing each dark wood surface with beeswax polish smeared on a soft yellow cloth. Then she would stand in the doorway, straighten her back, admire the sheen, the smell, the warmth and most of all the character — definite enough almost to seem incontrovertible — of the place she had created. She smiled, dusted her hands on the side seams of her jeans and began on another room.

There always *were* other rooms. At first they seemed empty, freshly-painted, echoing, floored with boards which creaked beneath the soles of her trainers. But soon enough, sure enough, they turned out to hold, under shrouds of sheets or in unpromising stacks against the walls, armchairs and armoires and paintings and porcelain sufficient to give the room — to allow Alice to give the room — its own beauty, entirely different from the last. Alice ticked off each room on her fingers as she finished it, with a sigh of satisfaction; she knew exactly what she'd achieved: and she knew there was more to come.

These, at night, were Alice's dreams.

But, during the days, who was she?

The question came to her — as it had several days running — as the dream cleared. It was morning. Mike was still asleep. She lay in bed probing the question and the panic beneath it, turning over the top layers in her mind, like soil, breaking them down into small particles so that — when she trod on the surface during the day — it would be familiar ground, not the treacherous minefield it always seemed first thing.

Everybody, she reasoned, ought to be able to go out into the world with a solid sense of self, to be able to say, 'I am like this . . . or that. I was like this (or that) yesterday. I'll be like it tomorrow and I'm like it today.' Why couldn't she?

No time to wonder. She slipped out of bed, into the bathroom and turned on the taps. As she watched the water gush, she thought: what she had been was one thing, what she might become was another. What came in between was the hard bit: harder still to justify it as a logical link between past and future. She stepped into the bath and splashed vigorously, soaped and sluiced behind her ears three times. Act positive, think positive, that was how to make an impression.

And wear the right clothes. She went back to the bedroom. Mike was snoring. She dressed in a short, navy blue skirt and tights and a purple cotton shirt and the thigh-length purple brocade jacket she'd saved for today. She inspected herself in the mirror, thrust her hands in her jacket pockets, her chin in the air. She left the flat.

At the Tube station, at the top of the static, litter-strewn escalator, there was a blackboard with a hand-written message. 'Essential Repairs', she read. Whoever had written the notice had added, 'Please help us to keep your station tidy.' A new meaning! 'You,' thought Alice. 'Pronoun, belonging to you. Also (colloq) belonging to a large corporation, but for which they wish the public to take some responsibility for daily maintenance.'

But this was not the kind of definition she would be required to come up with if — by any remote chance — she were successful. Holdman and Ray's, she knew from their catalogue, were makers of prescriptive dictionaries, which told how words should be used, not how they were; indeed they made much of their contribution to upholding traditional standards of language. Alice shook her head. Surely the only standard worth upholding was that of accuracy in recording how people used it? She wouldn't say that, though.

On the train she ran over in her mind the more obvious questions she might be asked and the answers she hoped were the right ones. She couldn't afford to play it by ear, be out of line, she must fit in. Just as, on her application form, she had fitted each of the random stages of her life into one or another of the boxes, presented each of them as a conscious step towards the goal of a job at Holdman and Ray's. Her years as a wordsmith were merely an apprenticeship in a related field, her months of living on the proceeds of Mike's stolen goods were self-directed home study.

Tottenham Court Road. She left the train.

Oxford Street. A young woman holding a clipboard stepped up to Alice.

'Would you like to receive a copy of a brand new fashion catalogue absolutely free?' she asked.

'What do I have to do?'

'Just answer a few questions.'

Alice checked her watch. She had time. She could use the practice. 'Okay.'

'Female,' answered Alice. 'Between 35 and 54. Single. Owner occupier. For over five years. Television. No car. *The Guardian. Cosmopolitan* occasionally. Over £15,000. Marks and Spencer's. Oxfam, Camden Lock, French Connection, Browns in South Molton Street if I could afford to. Nike's, but I've a pair of Nick's at the moment.' Alice grew more substantial as she spoke. For what a lot she had to say about herself and all of it true, except, of course, the salary; but who would admit to less than that?

The woman shuffled a sheaf of cards. 'Can you identify any products from these pictures?'

'No.' It was quite enough to identify herself.

Holdman and Ray's. In reception a young man in a dark suit sat on the edge of a green leather banquette, in the shadow of a large date palm. Alice smiled; he didn't smile back. She rang the bell on the counter. A woman appeared and said in a Sloaney voice, 'Oh, you're the ten-thirty.' (So that's who Alice was now.) 'They're running late. Haven't seen the ten o'clock yet. Take a seat,' and disappeared again.

Alice looked at the ten o'clock. He was probably a recent graduate and therefore ideal for such a junior job. The woman reappeared and beckoned him. Alice concentrated on tucking her stray thoughts into one or another of the boxes she remembered from the application form until it was her turn.

And then, there she was in the interview room, on a rather low upright chair.

On the other side of the shiny expanse of table sat a man and a woman, heads down, shuffling papers. Alice could see that the topmost of the man's papers was her application form; the topmost of the woman's papers was a new form, empty. She held her pen poised over it.

They raised their heads, welcomed Alice and asked her what she had to offer. Alice hadn't expected to be given free rein. She felt a surge of power like a blip on the national grid or like the roar when she switched on the hoover; only in this case the power generated an outpouring of ideas rather than an ingestion of dirt.

She spoke swiftly and surely, told them how she set about each definition, her methodical approach to the overall project, her ability to see a task — however large — through from start to finish. She talked knowledgeably of rival dictionary publishers, compared their wares critically with those of Holdman and Ray's. This last, she knew, demonstrated a knowledge and a capacity to analyse it well beyond what the post demanded.

As she spoke and as her words sounded increasingly confident, increasingly sensible in her own ears, her hands began to follow them, punctuating each point; opening outwards, palms up, for an expansive one; flattening the air, palms down, for a precise one; clasping, thumbs tight, for an earnest one; steepling, fingers pressed together, for a deliberate one.

She paused, brought her remarks to a close, sat back in her chair; and folded her hands neatly in her lap.

She looked at her prospective employers. The man wore

bifocals and had a week, receding chin. The woman had a sharp, thin little nose like a bird and sparse, crimped yellow hair. Neither of them were a patch on Alice, Alice decided.

'Tell me,' began the man, 'you seem very nervous. Why is that?'

Alice flipped back her hair and smiled with surprised confidence. 'Nervous?'

He nodded. 'Jumpy.' He waved his hands in a brief, sketchy parody of one of Alice's gesticulations, as though he hadn't the energy to copy her properly. 'Uncomfortable. Would you say you were uncomfortable?'

Alice suppressed a desire to shrug her shoulders, to fling up her arms on either side of her head. The gesture would be too exotic, too Latin, too exuberant for this tight-lipped pair. Besides, if they wanted her to keep her hands in her lap, she could keep her hands in her lap, no sweat.

'No.' Not moving an inch.

He tilted his face; the light caught his spectacles and reflected a malevolent gleam.

'Of course,' he informed her, 'you haven't actually worked before, have you?'

Not worked? What was this about? But of course, she decided, managing not to nod, this was one of those interview techniques, designed to put the candidate on the spot, to find out what she was made of.

'I was self-employed.'

'Hm. Do you think you'd be able to cope with the routine? Coming to work every day rain or shine? No taking a morning off when you felt like it?'

'To be self-employed,' Alice explained, patient, 'means to take sole responsibility for organising your time. It means working for results — and achieving those results — you can't stop just because you've put in the hours.'

The man's lip curled. He looked down at Alice's application. 'You were a wordsmith, I see, for a good many years.'

She nodded.

'Hardly an ideal background for a Holdman and Ray's lexicographer,' he judged. 'We don't expect creativity, what we want is good, sound, thorough attention to detail. And a workforce which keeps its nose to the grindstone.'

The woman, Alice noticed, was writing, filling in the boxes on the form before her.

'I've already explained,' said Alice, 'how essential I consider a meticulous approach. And how I've used it to good effect in the past.'

The woman was putting Alice's head in one box, her no longer gesticulating hands in another, her feet, one of which had begun to tap the floor, in a third.

'Ah yes,' said the man, 'and there's this dictionary you say you're compiling. What makes you feel you are qualified for such an undertaking?'

The woman wrote busily, transferring Alice onto the paper so that soon all of Alice would be chopped up and itemised and boxed away and there would be nothing left of the real Alice at all.

'It's an entirely separate project from any work I might do in this post. It proves, however, that I have all the skills set out in your description of the job.'

'Any work you *might* do?' the man raised thin, black eyebrows. 'How much work would you do, do you think?'

This was almost unanswerable. Yet, 'Nine to five, five days a week, to the best of my ability,' replied Alice.

His small eyes snapped. 'And you think that will be enough? Simply to put in the time?' He turned to the woman. 'Mrs Landsdowne?'

She stopped writing. She raised her peak-nosed face. Alice saw that there were deep, cartilaginous rings of wrinkles around the bulging column of her neck, like a tree trunk round, revealing its age. As she spoke, the wrinkles deepened.

'You said, Miss Mayer,' she said, 'that a thorough knowledge of spoken English usage was as important as a background in etymology. Why do you think that?'

But Alice knew by now that the woman already had her answer — Holdman and Ray's answer, the right answer — and no interest at all in hearing Alice's.

She mumbled something, she wasn't sure what.

'And could you speak up for Holdman and Ray's?' the woman persisted. 'As a representative of the firm. We do expect loyalty. Supposing you were called on to do that?'

But the job description had mentioned nothing of the kind. Alice, caught off guard, said so.

'So you would expect to work strictly according to the letter of the duties it sets out?' The woman left no pause for Alice to respond, but went on, 'Are you a *union member*, Miss Mayer?'

And then they were both at it, ripping at Alice, tearing chunks out of her, seizing the morsels, docketing them, fitting them into the boxes on the woman's form.

She wanted to rise, gather her dignity, leave. No, she wanted to turn and run. But she must sit still, squat in those boxes on the form.

'I dare say you've never worked with an Apple Mac,' said the man. 'It is a requirement.'

'At least two years' experience in a related field was what we specified,' said the woman.

'A degree in linguistics or similar,' the man added. 'I see you have only a City and Guilds.'

'This is, of course, a professional post,' said the woman. 'Not for someone with a background in one of the crafts.'

'A career position,' the man went on. 'We shall expect whoever we appoint to stay with us a minimum of five years.'

'And that would be a minimum,' the woman stressed. 'Most of our employees make a rather longer-term commitment.'

Alice could feel the job growing bigger and bigger; and she was growing smaller. The job was expanding so rapidly it filled the room, like ectoplasm, thick, foggy, impenetrable, ungraspable. Besides which, Alice was shrinking so rapidly she had little hope of grasping even the pencil in front of her. Ironic that, on the other side of the table, the man was talking about an effective grasp of something or other.

'Do you believe,' he asked, 'that you could offer something other candidates can't? That you can come up to our extremely high standards?'

Alice stared at him, eyes glazed. If she looked away she would only see the job, its duties expanding, creeping across the floor, filling every corner.

She was torn to shreds. She looked down at her lap. And there lay the pieces, strewn. Or was it a Kleenex she'd shredded?

'Mr Pettifer,' said the woman and smirked, 'any further questions?'

His glasses gleamed. 'Always gives cause for doubt when I come across someone who can't hold down a steady job.'

Hold down? thought Alice. She had as little chance of that as of preventing a great, flapping bird from taking off, of forcing a huge balloon filled with hot air, single-handedly, to the earth. She was becoming smaller and smaller, she could scarcely put her chin on the edge of the table now, she was so diminished.

'One final point,' the man persisted. 'I see you have a great many other interests. Are you going to be able to spare enough time for this post?'

And, pop! Alice disappeared.

She reappeared, God knew how much later, but in the same place and to find her interrogators talking to each other. They didn't seem to have noticed she'd been away — or that she had returned. They were talking to each other, arguing about the firm's policies on Learner Dictionaries. Was this a ploy? Had she still to be wary? They went on talking.

They stopped, rose and shook hands with Alice. They said they'd let her know. Let her know what? What was there left to know? What was there left?

On the Tube, Alice enumerated, as a mantra, a comfort, 'Female. Between 35 and 54. Single. Owner occupier. Over five years. Television,' but couldn't face mentioning, even silently, the idea of the fifteen thousand pounds a year.

By the time she arrived at Archway she wanted nothing more than to run down the road home, to go straight to the bathroom, to take the loo roll off the holder, begin crying as she carried it into the living room, settle in the armchair and weep, peeling paper from the roll as required; and stay there for hours until she transferred all the dampness in her head to the paper, flinging it, as she soaked it, onto the floor in wads. Until the armchair sailed on a sea of scrumpled loo roll. Until she had some idea who she was.

But before she could reach the bathroom, she was brought up short, in the hallway, by stacks of square, white cartons. She inspected them. There was a picture on the side of each: of a grotesque, rubbery face topped by a single tuft of synthetic black hair. 'Amaze your friends with Gordon the Grunt,' she read below one of the faces.

Distracted, she went into the living room where she found Mike watching TV. She stood behind him. Some programme about the treatment of the elderly in different states, by the sound of it. 'This is a better country not to be young in,' said a woman.

Alice thought there was something wrong with that. Not the grammar; the meaning was off-beam.

She shouldn't worry about it. Syntax was not her area except insofar as the arrangement of a group of words affected, contextually and as permanently as words could be affected, the meaning of a single word. And all the words in that sentence meant what they meant, their meanings were unchanged if you changed their order. Though if you changed the order, you did change the meaning. 'This is a better country to be not young in,' was surely what the woman meant?

'Mike,' said Alice. 'If Gordon is the Grunt, how would you describe me? In one word?'

He turned to look at her. 'You worry too much.'

'That's four. And they'll melt if you leave them in the hall.'

'What will?'

'The Gordons the Grunt,' said Alice. 'The central heating runs there. It's boiling underfoot. Are they knock-off?'

He shook his head. 'I've decided to go into something new. Novelties. Selling them.'

'I've just been for a job myself.'

Mike groped in the plastic carrier which lay at his feet and produced a cushion.

'I've no idea if I'll get it. I tried to make my background sound conventional.'

'Sit on this,' he instructed.

'It won't fart?' He shook his head. She put it on a chair and sat on it. It said: 'Worry, worry, worry, worry, worry.' Alice rose and it stopped.

'Ideal for you,' said Mike.

Alice said, 'If I did get it, I might be able to afford to publish my own dictionary.'

'Self employment,' said Mike. 'It's the only way. No one with a full-time job ever made a million.' He groped in the bag again.

'But this would be to finance my dictionary. Besides there's nothing to live on. You haven't brought in a penny recently.'

'Catch.' He tossed a rubber ball at her and, the instant it was in the air, it began laughing. Alice tossed it back. She laughed too. 'That's the idea,' Mike approved. 'One person buys it, then all his friends catch the bug. Perfect Christmas gift.'

'It's all very well,' said Alice, 'but someone has to earn something. You haven't any money.'

'Something else.' He took a video cassette from the bag. 'Are you watching this?' and waved a hand at the TV. Alice looked at the screen. A man in uniform, outside a prison, said, 'If an incident were to occur and could not be contained, then it might well spread.' Which of those words, in the context of that sentence, meant anything at all? Alice shook her head. 'Let's see what you've brought.'

He crossed to the video, then returned to his chair, carrying the remote control.

There was a great deal of crackling, followed by jiggling, tinny, music. Titles. Not in English. Swedish, Alice thought. A shot of a Gothic house (night-time exterior, towers) then (interior) of the hostess, a large woman in black, explaining, according to the subtitles, to her several guests that a clue to a treasure hunt was to be found in each room. 'This bit's silly,' said Mike and fast forwarded.

'Hang on,' said Alice.

He stopped. A man and a woman made a stagey search of a bedroom, then undressed each other. The man was dark and stocky with heavy thighs, large feet and love handles paunching over the top of each hip. The quality of the film was poor too; it was even hard to be certain, later, whether semen or visual interference besmattered the scene.

'Not much good?' asked Mike.

'Let's not make snap judgements,' said Alice.

She wondered, though, why she was watching. Ought she not to be concerned about the women who appeared in the film? About economic exploitation? About their picking up sexually transmitted diseases?

'Unusual angle,' said Mike. 'Cameraman must be a dwarf.'

And, as she *was* watching, ought she not to consider herself a feminist? Or to consider herself not a feminist?

Later, in the night, in her dreams, Alice returned to her house: this time to the one with the tower. As in every house, Alice set out to choose her room. But, as in every house, someone else had bagged the best ones first: had dumped a rucksack, a pile of books, a teddy bear on the bed as proof of ownership.

For yes, there *were* other people in the house — whichever house — hordes of them, part of a large family of which Alice was also a part.

During the day the members of this family invaded the kitchen (which Alice had already put straight); they snacked on the end of the long table, they grazed on crisps and peanuts from the cupboards, they raided the fridge for sandwiches and salads. And in the evenings they invaded the room — whichever room — that Alice had just finished and in which she was about to relax.

They brought with them many objects which Alice had not planned for the room: Pampers, some clean, some soiled; Fisher-Price garages inhabited by rotund peg-people who moved out, rolled under the sofa and stayed there; amputated yellow limbs of Garfields and disembodied manes of My Little Ponies; fluffy kittens which left damp, smelly patches; rancid trainers; later they brought loud CD players, raucous ghetto blasters, dirty coffee mugs, overflowing ash trays, stained wine glasses, crumpled Rizla papers, even the smeared mirrors on which they had cut their lines of coke. And they left them there.

But this time, in this dream, Alice had something new to look forward to, something special, something private, somewhere entirely her own: she had the tower room.

So Alice — while the rest of them swarmed into the room she had most recently transformed — climbed up and up the winding stone stairs, each with the centre scooped out by years — centuries? — of tramping feet; and stepped inside.

She stood close to the wall, where her weight would be less of a strain on rotten boards. She gazed at the room. As she had expected, it was circular. But she had not expected its beauty, apparent even in this decrepit state. The room was perfect.

It had been evening below, but it was morning here. Sun streamed through arched windows of stained glass, casting warm pools of vibrant light on the dusty floor. At the centre of the room was a great circular seat, canopied in red velvet, looped with hangings of rich brocade. She stepped towards it, testing her footing first. The floor held. She reached the centrepiece, bent to lift the hangings and discovered beneath them nothing: nothing but the sand-coloured, crumby, irregular ends of eaten-away planks.

She stepped back. Too late. The boards beneath her feet gave way. She gripped the hangings. They parted with a single, harsh sound. The tints of the stained glass whirled above her, round her, a rainbow of colour from which she fell, a spinning vortex of colour at the centre of which she plunged into black infinity.

Alice woke shouting. The light was on. Mike was leaning on one elbow, looking at her: 'What?' he said.

She shivered. 'I don't know who I am.'

'Weird.'

'I might be anyone. So might you.' She shook her head. 'Sorry, I meant . . . I was dreaming. I didn't where I was.'

'You're here.'

She looked around the bedroom. 'So I am.'

'So go to sleep.' He switched off the light.

Saturday. The catalogue arrived. Mike pushed off somewhere with his cartons of Gordon the Grunt.

Alice sat in the kitchen with a mug of coffee and looked at the pictures of the clothes she could buy with the £50 of instant credit she could have if she wanted. The swimsuits were ones with high, cutaway legs, modelled by Jerry Hall lookalikes: and she liked looking at them. Did this mean Alice was bisexual?

There was a knock at the door. She went to answer it.

A small, pale woman in a raincoat stood outside. 'Do you believe in the power of love?' she asked.

'No thank you,' said Alice.

'Could I just ask you? We are asking everyone. Do you believe Christianity to be a force for good or for evil?'

'Evil,' said Alice.

The woman stretched her face into a smile. 'We find that many people nowadays feel as you do. But if you read the Bible, you will discover God's message is quite different.'

'I have. I was brought up on the Bible. In the beginning was the word and all that.'

'Does this mean you're a Christian?'

'No. God should have stopped to think what people would do with the word.'

'But could I just ask you . . .?'

'No,' said Alice and shut the door. She returned to the kitchen. She closed the catalogue and picked up last week's *Mail on Sunday* magazine instead. She spotted a competition sponsored by Benson and Hedges. She studied it. Who did she have to be to enter?

The front door banged. Through the open kitchen door she watched Mike dump a pile of Gordon the Grunts in the hallway. 'No joy?' He nodded. 'Will be. Just a matter of finding the right market.' He joined her.

'What was that last night?' he asked. 'About not knowing who you were?'

'Don't ask me.'

'Why not?'

'Because too many people have recently. Anyway I've discovered who I am. I'm a resident UK smoker.'

'Since when?'

She tapped the *Mail on Sunday* mag. 'Since now.'

'Say,' he said, 'you went for a job in a no-smoking office?'

'I just have.'

'So you're a non-smoker, right?'

'That's like saying I didn't go to a single-sex school because I discovered afterwards that a classmate had a sex change in later life.'

'Did she?'

Alice shook her head.

'I've never seen you smoking,' he went on.

Alice rose and marched into the living room. On the mantelpiece she found a battered Dorchester packet with two bent cigarettes inside. She took one of them into the kitchen, rummaged in a drawer, found a box of matches and lit the cigarette. She coughed. 'I was born here,' she said. 'I live here. And I'm smoking, okay?'

He shrugged. 'Up to you. I've brought you something. Here.' He took a brightly coloured cardboard tube from his pocket.

'A kaleidoscope!' Alice stubbed out the stale cigarette.

'Mate of mine had a whole load. Do you know?' he went on, 'they've always only been marketed as toys? But designers use them to find new patterns for wallpaper and fabrics. That's what I thought I'd do with this one.'

'Let's have a look.' Alice held out her hand, but he raised the tube to his right eye, squinted and rotated the bit at the end. 'Amazing how they work,' he said.

'How do they?'

'Prisms. Two of them. I looked it up. At an angle of sixty degrees to each other. They reflect the bits of coloured glass at the end and then they reflect the reflections and so on and hey presto. That's why the patterns are symmetrical; and the number of patterns is infinite.'

'I thought it was for me,' Alice complained.

'Just a couple more goes. This one is something else. Is there a piece of paper handy?' She found one. 'It would be brilliant on a tee-shirt.' He squinted down at the paper, then back into the kaleidoscope. 'Damn. Gone. I'll never get it back.'

'Because of the number of patterns being infinite,' he explained. 'Same bits of glass all the time, but you see something different. And always a pattern.'

And as he spoke Alice saw she was not at the centre of the coloured vortex of the stained glass windows after all, was not plummeting out of it and into the dark; she was the vortex itself and the fragments of who she was were reflected over and over to make different patterns according to the light and the way the fragments fell. And she saw words flung up against each other, forming new patterns of meaning each time. Never the same, yet always the same — and always, every time you looked, complete and complex, even beautiful: and destined never to appear again, not quite in that exact configuration.

'Yes, I see,' she said. 'Now can I have a look?'

a glimpse into the future

Once upon a time, long ago, in the late nineteen fifties, when it was fashionable for women to have breasts like big, circle stitched zits, everyone — Miss Burrows included — was a great deal taller than Alice. They were so much taller that even in groups of eleven-and-twelve-year-olds, Alice walked in a forest of legs: from above which, occasionally, a large face would swoop to her level, jeer, then ascend again beyond visibility. But Miss Burrows, although she too swooped, casting Alice's desk into shadow, never jeered.

Alice was thinking about the fifties because she was looking at a Helmut Newton photograph in a glossy volume Mike had brought home; (Mike was going to be a photographer these days). The picture was of a curly-haired blonde woman, on a yacht, wearing a jaunty cap and a tight, white ribbed sweater which outlined the twin peaks of her breasts in their full enormity.

Enormous, yet not in the least mammary: not animal, certainly not fleshly. They seemed, collectively, a man-made superstructure, an expensive, padded penthouse whose style matched, but did not marry with, the original building. Was that effect a product of Newton's rather distasteful art? Alice wondered. Was it a consequence of the contrived pose (the woman was gazing unconvincingly out to sea)? Or was it, simply, that that's how women used to make their breasts look?

That's how Miss Burrows's looked. Great, looming, upholstered bulks jutting across Alice's desk with Miss Burrows's voice issuing from lips unseeable above the promontory.

What colour bulks? Pale blue, baby blue; probably cashmere, Alice surmised and probably part of a twinset. Miss Burrows leaned over them and smiled. Her lips were cherry red, she smelt of face powder, her pale hair was curled into sausagey rolls around her face and at the nape of her neck, but pressed flat at the back of her head. When Miss Burrows left school in the afternoon, she fitted a small, crisp, black hat over the flat section of her hair and secured it with long pins as though she were driving them through her skull.

What had happened to Miss Burrows? Was she still married to that Gerald man? Alice decided to write care of her old school and find out.

But first she would look for that photograph of Miss Burrows's wedding.

It wasn't, when she found it, at all as she remembered. Miss Burrows was not a period-piece schoolmistress, but a small, pretty, contented-looking, thirtyish woman; the Gerald man was not a terrifying ogre, but tall, rather mild-faced and wearing an army uniform; and there was a flock of small bridesmaids, all smiling, apart from Alice who frowned grimly at someone or something outside the picture.

Someone or something real? Imagined? Alice wrote her letter, pausing between the lines to remember the strange dreamy life she lived as a child, a life peopled by creatures beckoning from outside the frame of her own world. Or from within the frame of theirs. Characters from picture books — The Flower Fairies of the Summer, elves, hobgoblins, a magician bending low over a tome, muttering 'the spell, the spell', tracing the words with his fingers; Uncle Tom Cobley appearing from the mist with his skeletal grey mare 'when the wind whistles cold on the moor of a night'. Some of them stepped off the pages into Alice's mind and accompanied her through her days; others stepped out, extended a hand and took her into the picture, then tripping lightly out of it — but into the world of it, like the real Alice in the looking glass world.

Alice finished her letter, stuck it in an envelope and found a stamp. She'd grown up with these glimpses into other worlds, a door opening just a chink, a flaw widening to a crack. Light, movement, noise rushing through the gap, but for a few seconds only like a car passing at high speed, one window open, music blaring. Other worlds.

She set off for the post box. Those other worlds, she thought as she strode along the pavement, were the reason one was not supposed to tread on the cracks between the flagstones. It was nothing to do with bears; it was because they might open up.

And the past, she nodded to herself as she dropped her letter into the slot, was another world too, a world just outside the frame of the photograph of Miss Burrows's wedding. What would it be like to go back into it?

She returned home. 'More boxes!' she said to Mike in the hall. 'Is it all off the back of a lorry?'

He shook his head. 'Photographic stuff going cheap. Managed to get the trays, the enlarger, the lamp, the lot. I'm going to set up in the cellar,' and disappeared into it.

Alice wondered if she could start an argument about this; it was her cellar; and life was uneventful just now.

But the following week, on Saturday, a pale green envelope arrived. It was addressed to Alice in a neat, round script. Alice opened it. It was a letter from Miss Burrows! She was still married to Gerald! After more than thirty years! Alice rushed around the flat looking for Mike.

Eventually she banged on the cellar door. A sliver of red light showed beneath it. Slow movements within. She explained at the top of her voice.

'They're still married!' She seized the door handle and tugged. 'They ought to be in the *Guinness Book of Records*.' The chink widened.

'Don't come in,' cried Mike. 'I'm developing.'

Alice closed the door and hung around outside for a while, holding the pale green paper. Mike didn't come out. He didn't come out for hours. When he did and joined her in the living room, he said, 'Lots of people stay married till they die. They're supposed to. It's in the wedding service.'

'Not people I know. They've all been through their copy of *How to Do Your Own Divorce in England and Wales* at least once.'

'Not people of that age. Why do you want to see your old teacher?'

'It might be instructive. What were you developing?'

'Technique.'

'I wonder what they're like now,' said Alice.

Elizabeth and Gerald were, in fact, very like each other, had grown like each other, they had been together so long. They both had sparse, soft grey hair, wore sensible shoes, mud-coloured clothes and their faces were pink-cheeked, fresh, open, lined only by age, not turbulence. 'Nice couple,' thought the postman, catching his usual glimpse of them at breakfast through the bungalow's french windows.

'Fifteen down,' said Gerald into his crossword from behind his *Telegraph*. 'I'm a muddled cleaner.'

Elizabeth folded her *Express*, laid it on the table, cleared the breakfast things and carried them into the kitchen.

'Gerald?'

He looked up. Elizabeth stood in the kitchen doorway, smiling that sweet contented smile of hers. It had been the contentment, the innocence of the smile — its tantalising contrast to her figure — which had first attracted him. He recalled with the vividness of reality one of their earliest evenings together in the darkness of the Roxy, Elizabeth's eyes fixed on Harry Belafonte, his on those wonderful breasts which he could not — not yet — touch. And he recalled with equal clarity a subsequent evening at her parents' home, the two of them alone together on the sofa: when he did touch them.

'Yes, dear,' he said.

She was holding a letter. 'It's from my ex-pupil Alice again. She's planning to come and see us.'

'Alice Mayer,' she prompted. 'You remember her?' He nodded again, though he still didn't. He wondered if Elizabeth shared his own memories. 'The smallest bridesmaid,' she went on. 'Pretty child, very imaginative, always so bright and cheerful. She seems to have done very respectably for herself, just taken a post with Holdman and Ray's. And she's planning to publish her own dictionary.'

'Might be able to help me with the crossword,' he said and went back to it.

Later, after Elizabeth set out with her basket on her arm, Gerald crossed to the french windows and looked out. At the small lawn, edged by shrubs, the patio. He sighed. The bungalow was ideal for people of their age and so was the garden, very little maintenance. He wished for a moment that the garden could be a bright sea of colour; but that would mean annuals, and all that potting out and weeding was too much. Or perhaps he just wished for some sign of life in the neat, green landscape.

He wondered whether he shouldn't have a dog; but it was too late, their lives were so settled and a dog would only make a mess all over Elizabeth's kitchen. Probably jump up on the sofa with his paws all muddy, the little beggar, he thought, chuckling; and in his mind's eye a liver-and-white springer spaniel nosed out from behind the rhododendrons and ran across the patio. Gerald went into the kitchen, took his weatherproof jacket from its hook and picked up his stout stick. The imaginary dog scratched at the door. He opened it and bent to fondle ears draggled with moisture. 'Better not let her catch you in here looking like that, old chap,' he warned and they went out together into the silent, leafy street for Gerald's morning walk.

Elizabeth bought chops for lunch and green peas: she'd make an apple pie for after, Gerald loved her pastry. The shopping over, she turned along the High Street, away from home. No hurry this morning, she had plenty of time and would still be back before Gerald expected her. Dear Gerald. They had such a comfortable life, with so many small pleasures — their meals together, their trips to the library, their Sunday excursions in the car, even the quiet contentment of sitting side by side by the fire; and lately there had been that wildlife series they both enjoyed so much she always planned their supper round it. They shared such a lot, always had. But there was one thing Elizabeth never shared.

She stopped at the familiar shop front with its red logo, its panelled-over window at the centre of which was the familiar picture of Desert Orchid, his noble grey head outstretched as he passed the post. She brushed aside the red and green plastic strips from the doorway and stepped in.

This time of day the shop was almost empty. It would be different later, Elizabeth knew — she had slipped in several times after a visit to the library or after telling Gerald she'd catch him up, because she'd forgotten to buy teacakes, a Swiss roll, a Battenburg.

Later the room would be crowded with men leaning on the counters round the walls. The air would be thick with cigarette smoke and excitement. On the TV screens the sleek, muscled horses sloped round the paddock, then cantered to the starting gate, quarters bunched, the bright silks of their jockeys' shirts fluttering in the wind. And they were off!

The young woman looked up as Elizabeth let the plastic strips fall behind her. 'Here she is again,' she thought. 'Poor old thing.

Probably all on her own. Comes in here just to have a few words.
Either that or she's short of a bob or two.'

'Five pounds to win on Bright Dreamer in the three-fifteen at
Doncaster,' said Elizabeth crisply. She handed over the money
and left.

Bright Dreamer, she reflected as she strolled back along the
High Street, showed good form according to this morning's
Express. But it wasn't the winning which mattered; it was the
picture she carried with her all day of her horse (grey like darling
Desi), the horse who in turn carried her hopes and her money all
the way in the horse box from Newmarket — or in this case
Lambourn — and onto the track. It was a real horse, strong-
smelling, head tossing when she buried her face in its mane; it
was the pony she had never owned.

Mike was getting on Alice's nerves. The pictures he wanted to
take were a nuisance. He didn't want to take pictures of people,
wasn't on the look out for the tiny gesture, the lift of the
eyebrow, the half-smile which would transform, eludicate a
lurching Holloway drunk. Mike wasn't interested in casting new
light on reality; he was interested in effect.

He spent ages arranging Alice and draping her: with a white
pac-a-mac she must have bought on some seaside holiday, with
several metres of slippery red jersey she'd intended to turn into a
dress; and with a quantity of black lace he must have acquired
for the purpose. He was very insistent about arranging the folds
so they fell right, made the best of contrasts with the tone of her
skin. He became very demanding about the way she moved. He
made her sit in odd positions which he said created interesting
planes of light and shade. He illuminated her, with her

anglepoise, from several different aspects. He took to calling, 'Hold it. Exactly like that,' while she was stepping out of the bath or standing with one leg in her jeans, one out.

'Mike,' said Alice, when he prevented her from removing a pan of brussels sprouts from the stove because the steam from the boiling water offered an interesting contrast to the contours of her outstretched arm, 'Mike, please stop.'

'In a tic. You couldn't put your arm *over* the steam?'

'No I couldn't. Mike you're not interested in me as a person any more.'

'Of course I am. Don't move.'

She did. 'I'm just an object, an image in the lens. I might as well,' she cast around the kitchen for a suitable comparison, 'I might as well be . . .' her eyes fell on the salt packet, ' a pillar of salt. Like Lot's wife. That was probably God's way of taking a snap. Turning a woman into a static lump.'

'If you could just put your hand back for a moment.'

'Mike, tomorrow I'm going on my trip.'

'All the more reason to let me get this right. It's not so much the angle,' he explained, 'it's more a question of the frame, the context in which the image appears.'

Frames. The windows of a train were frames of a kind, Alice supposed, as she sat looking out of one onto London's grey southern suburbs. But the pictures they held were unalluring. She thought instead of Mike imprisoned of his own free will in the cellar, sweating, she imagined, in the small space under the light of his red lamp. She'd been going, before he was so heavily into photography, to ask him if he'd like to come with her, 'Just,' as she would have put it had she asked, 'for the ride'.

What was Mike's attraction, she wondered? He was a popular character these days, she only had to look about her to see that. Not Mike as Mike, but Mike as person — the lovable Cockney rogue like Dennis Waterman or what's his name who played Boon. Middle-class women were supposed to fall for this type; they did on TV. Were she and Mike, then, a cliché of the 1990s? If so, what did that say about the world? And what had happened to New Man? He'd seemed to have so much going for him, yet he'd only lasted a few measly years. Fashions in men changed so quickly it was hard to envisage how Miss Burrows had survived with just the one Gerald throughout all these years. She must be unhappy — Alice nodded to herself — but remained with him from either inertia or necessity.

Or maybe, just maybe, they were happy together? And maybe this trip into Alice's past would also give her a glimpse of the future?

The train was drawing into the station. She picked up her bag.

Outside, a thin, spiteful drizzle fell in the darkening afternoon. Alice looked at the sky; the weather did not promise well for the walk on the downs she had planned for the morning.

She climbed a flight of steps and was in the street, a narrow street with even narrower pavements. Cars sped past as though on a through road. To her left a Belisha beacon shed its meagre, intermittent glow on the shiny wet tarmac. To the right was the town. Not much to look at. It was tiny, no more than a spidery-shaped blotch in a dip in the wide grey sweep of the downs. She set off for the centre.

A crossroads. A clock tower. Long low brick terraces; those which were still houses had no front gardens; most had been converted into shops, tastelessly.

She found her b & b, left her bag in her room and set off again in search of a restaurant.

After an early dinner Alice walked once more along the main street. She considered entering one of the cramped little pubs, but she didn't want to be a stranger in a roomful of regulars. If Mike had come with her, then the others would have been strangers, she and he could have commented on them, even made jokes. But would they? She and Mike weren't a society in themselves, as some couples seemed to be. They gave each other — that was it! — no security. Sometimes, she thought, it might be nice to be one half of a comfortable pair. She turned off the High Street up a narrow lane. The drizzle drifted under the hood of her anorak.

Some householders had not yet drawn their curtains. Each window was a bright square of warmth, a window on the warmth of a family, a world of comfort. In each world, in a place of prominence, stood the bright, flickering square of the television, holding the family immobile by its mobility. Alice kept walking.

Come to think of it, she was better off outside. The bright warmth was an attraction when she could see only part of it, imagine the rest. Inside, it would be familiar, enclosed claustrophobic; inside it would be the square of unknown dark beyond the window which would be inviting. There would be more to choose from out there.

Between some of the houses were gaps which opened into even narrower lanes with even smaller houses or, under arches, into cobbled yards whose surrounding stables and hay lofts had been converted into flats. Unnoticed, Alice peered into the gaps, under the arches. How close people lived in this town. Yes, she was glad she was out here; and tomorrow she wanted to be off on her own.

Her morning walk, though wet, went well. She returned refreshed, changed into dry clothes and set out for The George, to which she had invited Miss Burrows and Gerald — ('Of course, I want to see you both') — for afternoon tea. She thought when she wrote that, that they would enjoy the outing; then decided — too late to do anything about it — that she had patronised them.

Her first thought was correct. A tea at The George was not to be sneezed at, not by Elizabeth and Gerald, especially as they didn't often indulge. Often enough, however, to know that there would be a choice of scones and hot buttered teacakes, would be slices of cherry-rich Genoa and a plate of fancies oozing real, fresh, dairy cream.

Alice arrived early and chose a table in the bow window from which she could watch them arrive, see them before they saw her. She wanted to peer out at them as she had peered in at families the night before, to catch them unawares wearing their real expressions, showing their real feelings for each other. Most of all she wanted to catch them seeming happy.

She recognised them the instant they turned the corner. Miss Burrows still had those big breasts, though the rest of her body had thickened to put them in proportion. As she came nearer, Alice saw she still had that open, soft, fresh face with contentment stamped all over it. And as the couple reached the steps to the door of The George they turned and smiled at each other warmly and — Alice decided — with real affection. So they were happy after all!

Alice was not to know that the smiles were of anticipation for the cream tea to come.

•

Somewhere in another world, perhaps even in another part of West Sussex, a tall grey horse lowered its head and whiffled softly, with love, through its nose at the liver-and-white springer spaniel sitting, ears alert, tail wagging, before it on the grass: but not among the rhodondendrons of Elizabeth and Gerald's garden.

having a wonderful time

Alice watched Timothy open the *Daily Telegraph*; he folded it neatly, ran his hand down the edge of the page to make a sharp crease and spread the paper on his desk. Then he unwrapped a packet of sandwiches and ate as he read. Fiona took her *Daily Mail* in one hand and dipped a teaspoon into a plastic carton of salad with the other. Neither Timothy nor Fiona spoke. For twenty minutes Alice crumbled crispbread with her fingers so as not to make a noise; she left her packet of ready-salteds untouched. Finally she rose, went to the small cupboard in the corner of the office, hefted the electric kettle, switched it on, cleared her throat and announced, 'I'm making coffee.'

Fiona said from behind her *Mail*, 'It's 10p each time. You put it in the tin.'

'I didn't mean that,' said Alice. 'I meant, would either of you like a cup?'

Timothy looked up at her through pebble glasses. 'Usually we make our own.'

'If you're boiling the water anyway, I'd prefer tea,' said Fiona. 'The Earl Grey is mine. I have it in the blue cup and saucer.'

'Next to the cup-a-soups, which is what I want,' explained Timothy. 'My name's on the packet.'

Alice rummaged in the cupboard, then stopped and turned. 'Can I ask you something?' No one answered. 'I just wondered,' she went on, 'if you bring your own things and only add water, why do you pay 10p each each time?'

'For the Christmas meal, of course,' said Timothy. He placed his sandwiches carefully on his desk. 'As a matter of interest,' he rose and crossed the room to the cupboard, 'I wonder how much is in the kitty now?' He picked up the coffee tin (which was actually a toffee tin), carried it back to his desk, tipped out the coins and began to count them. Alice poured water into three cups and took one to Fiona, one to Timothy. 'Where do you go for the meal?' she asked.

'Thanks. Different places.' He sighed. 'I suppose we'll have the usual problem of finding somewhere we all like. Rosemary will try to insist on Chinese or Indian again, I dare say.'

'Wherever we choose Henry will sit in the corner nodding and looking as though he wished he were at the pub round the corner.' Fiona screwed up her face.

'Oh well.' Timothy took a sip of soup. 'At least Douglas always seems to have a good time.'

'Douglas! He was responsible for last year's fiasco. That dreadful Berni Inn. Those crackers. The paper hats. Douglas actually wore his.'

'At least they served a proper dinner. The place you suggested, I didn't recognise a single thing on the menu. You wouldn't get a proper dinner there. And the prices!'

'Brules is extremely good value for what it is. Excellent

service. Nice people. Remember that drunken man who bothered me last year?' Timothy shook his head. 'Well, you wouldn't come across anyone like that in Brules.'

'Even if I liked foreign food, it wouldn't like me. Mother says the men in our family are all the same. Proud stomachs.'

'Proud stomachs! Honestly I don't know why we bother.'

'Why do you?' Alice chipped in. They both stared at her. 'Bother, I mean. If you all prefer different meals, wouldn't it be better to split the money and go to different places?'

'Go out to dinner on my own?' Fiona stopped spooning salad. 'Suppose someone saw me? And besides, this is the office party.'

Timothy nodded and balanced the last coin carefully on top of a neat pile. 'It's nice to have some sort of a do,' he explained. 'As long I can have a proper dinner.' He looked up. 'We've roughly fifty pounds here. That's not enough for all of us. We'll need a levy.'

The office door flew open, then banged shut. 'Levy for what?' demanded Rosemary. She strode across the room and flung her leather jacket over the back of her chair. 'Have you lot finally understood the value of the fighting fund? And about time too. Supposing we were sacked or laid off? We'd be left without a penny, the way things are.' She wrenched at her desk drawer. 'I have the forms. You just sign the declaration.' 'Actually,' Timothy said, 'we were talking about the Christmas party.'

'Oh that.' She shrugged. 'Make sure you choose somewhere that has access for wheelchairs this time, that's all I ask.' 'Wheelchairs?' asked Alice. 'Who's going in a wheelchair?' 'Don't be dense.' Rosemary glared at her. 'It's a matter of principle. We shouldn't patronise places without disabled access. If everyone did that, they'd provide ramps soon enough. Are you going to sign one of these, or not?' Alice nodded. 'And while you're about it have you filled in your application to join the NUJ?'

Henry shuffled in, hung up his coat and moved swiftly and silently to his desk. Timothy announced, 'I've recounted, to be on the safe side. I make it forty-nine pounds and seventy-three pence. Plus twenty pesetas. Who put those in?' 'We all know who goes to Benidorm every summer,' said Fiona.

Douglas appeared in the doorway. He grinned. 'Not Benidorm. Torremolinos.' Timothy said, 'We were discussing the office party.' Henry muttered. 'A bit more work and a bit less chat; that's what we need around here,' and everyone went to his or her desk.

Henry's desk is to the left of Alice's. Henry is very old and bald and his chin has sunk almost to his collarbone: from years and years hunched over the small print, Alice supposes. All morning she has listened to him read aloud, slowly and distinctly, into a tiny tape recorder. He read, 'March, cap M, Monday, Cap M, bold, 27. 86–279, Week 13, Cap W, Easter Monday, Cap E, Cap M, Holiday, cap H. Open brackets, UK, cap U, cap K, comma except Scotland, Cap S, close brackets.' And so on.

Now he switches on his tape recorder, rewinds the tape and listens to the machine repeat his morning's words as he checks them against his proofs.

As for Alice, she sits in front of a computer screen and tries to decide whether timber means 'cut wood' or 'wood for building'; this section of Holdman and Ray's produces dictionaries as well as diaries and Alice is working on an ELT dictionary for native speakers of Swahili. 'Wood for building,' she decides and taps it on her keyboard. Alice hopes she has made the right decision; it is her first day at Holdman and Ray's.

Alice defines 'timbre' next. The afternoon wears on. Sometimes Henry reaches something out of the ordinary — Septuagesima, Lammas or Fifteenth after Trinity. Alice likes the sound of these; they have a romantic ring to them and they come as a surprise — though Henry, of course, must know exactly when they will turn up.

Then Alice considers the meaning of time — partly because of Henry's monologue and partly because it is the next word she has to define. 'There's doing time,' she thinks, 'there's having a good time, giving someone a good time, and there's sparing the time. So time means prison, fun, sex and attention.' But the dictionary is to have a vocabulary of 2,000 words max and requires only the simplest of explanations. Alice is giving time more attention than it needs.

She sighed and checked her watch. 'What is time?' she wondered out loud. Douglas replied, 'Nearly half past four. POETS.'

'What?'

'POETS: push off early, tomorrow's Saturday. I am for one.' He switched off his computer, then leant towards her. 'Don't suppose you fancy a quick one,' he suggested, 'to celebrate the end of your first week? Just at the pub round the corner, no big deal . . .'

'Day,' said Alice, 'A day doesn't count as a week.' She added quickly, 'I would have started on Monday but they told me it had to be the first of the calendar month,' then realised Douglas was waiting for an answer. 'Sorry, thanks, it's very nice of you; but I have to be somewhere else.'

It wasn't true. Strap-hanging on the Tube home, Alice allowed herself to wonder how long she'd last at Holdman and Ray's. The work was boring, her colleagues unfriendly and she hated sitting in a room with other people all day long. She reminded herself that she had no option but to stick it out. It was no good dreaming about those idyllic days when she lived comfortably at home with Mike on the proceeds of stolen goods. On the other hand, why worry about her new colleagues for the moment? She didn't have to face them again till Monday. More important was how to get through the weekend alone.

The thing to do, she decided, was to make a start on some positive project. Clean the flat? No, too energetic. Decorate the flat? No, far too big an undertaking. What about the washing? Yes, that was it.

At Archway she left the train, ran up the escalator, hurried down the street, ducked into the supermarket where she bought a large box of Persil Automatic, rushed out again and scurried along the road to her flat. She let herself in, switched on the hall light, tossed her coat over a chair, switched on the living room light, the kitchen light and the bedroom light, then stripped the bed. She sorted the whites from the coloureds, the colourfasts from those which ran, stuffed the sheets into the Hotpoint, measured the powder and selected the cycle. She started the machine and the kitchen was filled with a companionable whooshing as water poured into the drum.

What next? She watched the water rise inside the machine. She fetched a sponge and wiped the glass door so she would have a clearer view. The water crept over the fabric which changed to a darker shade and slowly sank beneath the tide. The drum began to churn. But what was that? Damn. Something bright green among the pale pink sheets. How could she have been so careless? But no, it was all right; she recognised it for what it was — a completely colourfast handkerchief.

Alice watched the washing being washed for an hour and

then she watched it being dried. The drying was a great deal more interesting because she could see the sheets and pillow cases change, gradually, from thudding wet lumps to free-floating fabric. She also enjoyed the diversion of the green handkerchief. Could she predict how frequently it would turn up, she wondered?

She checked her watch and found that the handkerchief's revolutions were irregular. Why was that? Was it because, as the sheets dried, they weighed less and therefore everything went round at a different rate? The machine clicked and its contents slowed, then flopped, like dying creatures, for the last time. Alice went to bed, where she was cold; she had been so busy with the washing machine she had had no time to put on a clean sheet or duvet cover.

On Saturday Alice did the same thing, only this time with a dark wash and a pale yellow shirt. The dark clothes would run, she knew, but what the hell? she'd never liked that shirt. Alice made herself comfortable with a cushion on the floor in front of the machine and ate her meals down there while she watched. How did the washing machine work exactly, she asked herself. Was it something to do with centrifugal force?

On Sunday she determined to restrict herself to a single cycle and to ration her viewing time; she ought to iron some of the clean clothes. But at the end of the first cycle she suddenly thought, 'I'm thirty-seven years old and I'm spending my weekend watching the washing go round.' A wave of nausea swept over her; she rushed into the bedroom, gathered another load, rushed back and stuffed it into the drum. But she still felt queasy.

She watched the washing and tried to think sensibly.

What, she asked herself, did she want out of life now that

Mike had left? What she needed, she decided, was someone to talk to. If only she hadn't lost touch with Sue and Lawrence. If only she had a party to go to. She shook her head. No, a party was not at all what she had in mind. All that bright, determined talk.

If she needed to talk, perhaps she should hire someone to talk to — a professional counsellor, a therapist? But if this was what she decided to do, where would she find the money to pay?

She sighed, abandoned the problem and returned to the kitchen. The last wash had been a mistake. She must have thrown in her shocking pink shirt in the rush to start the machine because everything had turned pink; everything apart from one pair of grey trousers. She sighed again. Might as well iron her new pink wardrobe.

In the morning Alice dressed in the grey trousers, the pink shirt, matching pink socks and pink sneakers. She pulled on a pink cotton jacket which had once been beige and made for the door.

There was a white envelope lying in the hall. Unusual. Of late, she received only brown ones. She picked it up and tore it open. It was a left-over from long ago; it was a royalty cheque. For a small amount but big enough, Alice judged, to make it worth phoning to see how much a counsellor would cost.

When she arrived at work Henry was already hunched over his desk. 'Good morning,' said Alice. 'Coronation Day, Caps, open brackets 153 dash 212 close brackets Saturday, Caps, good morning,' said Henry.

Alice switched on her computer. Whoever produced the first draft of this dictionary had no imagination at all, she decided. He or she had defined 'timid' as 'lacking courage'. Alice asked herself what the word meant and came up with a picture of a small, brown creature, whiskers a-twitch, peeping out of a hole into a huge and frightening world. She changed the definition to 'mouselike'.

'Morning, all,' breezed Douglas. 'Staff shortages on the Victoria Line again.' He took his seat, then turned to Alice. 'My, my, we are in the pink today, aren't we?' 'I like pink,' replied Alice firmly.

She was hard at work on 'toil', when Fiona came over with a piece of paper. Alice took it and inspected it. It was headed 'Dictionaries and Diaries Christmas meal'. Underneath was the query 'Lunchtime or evening?' Everyone else had ticked 'evening', so Alice did the same. But there were other decisions to be made and none of them anywhere near so easy. She had to choose a date, indicate any dates she couldn't make, suggest a venue, say what kind of food she preferred and whether she liked a place with background music or somewhere they could dance. The final query was whether she had any special dietary requirements.

'Fish or chicken only, no red meat,' someone had written. 'Turkey with trimmings,' that must be Timothy. 'Somewhere decent — Kensington or Chelsea preferably.' (Fiona?) 'Hackney's the best place for Turkish. Or there's a Goan restaurant near King's Cross, bring your own booze.' 'Anywhere, so long as it has no loud music.' 'Somewhere with dance music.' 'A pub that does food on the side?' 'A wine bar?' 'A steakhouse?' 'French cuisine, if poss.' 'Not Chinese food. Not a pub. Certainly not the one round the corner.'

Then there was the matter of which day. 'Friday before Christmas,' someone had written. 'TRAVEL are having their do then and I'll be too pissed to enjoy ours,' someone else had responded. 'The Wednesday before?' suggested a third party. 'Can't. Yoga class,' retorted a fourth.

Alice sighed. She couldn't even read quite a bit of the writing because somebody — Douglas, she suspected — had drawn doodles of plum puddings and bells and sprigs of holly all around the edges. She thought for a moment, then wrote 'vegetarian' in tiny letters on the small space left at the bottom of the page and handed the questionnaire to Henry who was next on the list.

At twelve-thirty precisely, Henry switched off his tape recorder; Douglas switched off his computer; Rosemary Oliver put on her leather jacket and announced, 'I'm off to see the Branch Secretary.'

'Oh no, you're not.' Timothy rose, crossed the room, stopped at her desk and flung a piece of paper onto it. 'You're not going anywhere.' He rounded on Douglas and Henry. 'Nor are you two. You can jolly well stay here.'

Everyone gazed at him. He jabbed a finger at the paper. 'I go to all that trouble drawing up this questionnaire so that we can enjoy ourselves,' he went on. 'And what do you do?'

No one moved. 'You treat it as though it doesn't matter — that's what.' He removed his glasses, thrust a hand into the pocket of his cardigan and drew out a large white handkerchief. 'You don't make any serious suggestions. What's more,' he wiped his glasses slowly, then settled them on his nose, 'you even deface it.' He replaced the handkerchief in his pocket and confronted them. 'It's not on. We'll sit here and discuss this properly right now. Or,' he paused, 'I'm not going to do any more of the organising. And I don't just mean for this year.'

Henry mumbled something about it not being anything to do with him. Rosemary protested that she had to go, she was expected. Fiona said she didn't see why she had to put up with this. Then Douglas objected that he had to have food and

Timothy announced, 'You have fifteen minutes to go and buy something. The rest of the lunch hour we sit down and we talk.'

Once outside, Alice headed for a call box. She phoned seven therapists before she found one she could afford and who had an hour free that evening. The woman couldn't be much good, she thought, if she wasn't booked up, but she would be better than nothing. So she made an appointment and hurried back to the office. Timothy was furious with her for taking so long, but she said, 'I agree with whatever you've all decided,' and took a back seat while the discussion went on around her.

That evening Alice had some difficulty finding the therapist; her office was in a tiny street south of the Mile End Road. When Alice finally discovered the building it confirmed her suspicions; it was decidedly tatty. And inside, the consulting room was less of a room, more of a cubicle, small and windowless. It held a low table with an ash tray and a box of Kleenex and, on either side of it, two upholstered chairs. The therapist sat in one, Alice sat in the other.

'Now,' the therapist began. She made a steeple of her hands. 'Call me Helen, by the way. Now, Alice, the first thing I always tell people is, it's perfectly all right to cry in here.' She gestured at the Kleenex.

'I don't want to cry.'

'Yet you said on the phone that you were unhappy.'

Alice thought. 'Not really unhappy. I was in a hurry, it was lunchtime. Sad would be a better word, I meant sad.'

'What seems to you to be the difference?'

'Well,' Alice thought again, 'unhappy people top themselves or slash their wrists. But when you're sad you're just sad, you don't do anything drastic. Sad also means sated, means that you've had enough, though that usage is no longer common.' She shook her head. 'I shall have to go back and redefine it.'

'Go back and do what?'

'I'm a lexicographer. I'm writing a dictionary. But someone else did the esses.'

'Was there any incident in particular which caused this feeling?'

Alice nodded.

'Do you want to tell me about it?'

Alice shook her head.

'Okay. Fine. Can you remember when you were last happy?'

She shook her head again.

'What would you say makes most people happy?'

'Well, they get off on getting together and dancing and eating and listening to music and maybe drinking too much.'

'Do you?'

'No,' said Alice and burst into tears.

She cried for ages. Helen said this wasn't a waste of Alice's money; she said it was a good start. Then Alice's time was up and she had to take several deep breaths and stop crying. She went home and took out a pile of clean clothes and stayed up late watching them being washed.

But, in a way, what Helen said was true. During the debates on Tuesday and Wednesday and Thursday lunchtimes, at several moments in the hours of tedium between and late in the evenings when the drying cycle was over, Alice had only to think of the box of Kleenex for her to feel better.

On Friday she had another appointment. As soon as she was seated in front of Helen with the tissues in her lap she began to cry. 'It's the office party,' she sobbed. 'It means so much to all of them. I can't bear it.'

'You mean they're all having a good time preparing for it and you're not?'

'No, no.' Alice shook her head and dried her eyes. 'They're not having a good time. They argue about it every day. They're horrible to each other.'

'And how are they towards you?' asked Helen, but Alice ignored her.

'On Tuesday,' she wept, 'they spent the whole hour arguing about the date. On Wednesday they went on and on about whether they wanted a place where they could dance. Douglas suggested the ravers could go on somewhere else afterwards, but Timothy said that wasn't the point; they had to find a place where everyone would have a good time. And Douglas nodded and said that when you thought about TRAVEL . . . just going to the pub.

'They were on the point of agreeing to go to a Greek restaurant near Sadler's Wells which does a traditional Christmas dinner on request and has dancing to live music later when Henry piped up. He said it was all humbug, and what had happened to the true spirit, the real meaning of Christmas . . .? He said what was the world coming to when young people wanted to go to a foreigners' place? They all rounded on him and accused him of not listening, he could have turkey there if he wanted, but he shook his head and said he wasn't talking about himself, he was talking about them and why did they have to be different just for the sake of it? Then Timothy said if people had their own ideas about what they enjoyed that was their affair, and Rosemary said was Sadler's Wells a convenient area anyway, and reminded them all that not everyone might be able to afford a taxi home. Then they launched into a discussion of whether some of the money should be used to pay for taxis and, if so —

this was Rosemary's suggestion — whether there should be a sliding scale of subs with those on the lowest pay receiving the full taxi fare and those who earned more being given only a proportion. After that they all demanded to know each other's take-home pay. Henry wouldn't say, but apart from him, it turned out that I was the poorest. And then they all glared at me. Rosemary especially.'

'How did you feel when they glared at you?'

'Fine,' said Alice. 'Well not necessarily. How should I know? The point is that on Friday, today, that is, Douglas said he'd been thinking about it overnight and maybe Henry had a point. It wasn't that he — Douglas that is — wanted to eat turkey, but he did think the atmosphere should be Christmassy. Would it be in this place? Would there be decorations? And a tree? He suggested that Fiona phone and find out. Fiona said why didn't he do it himself? Douglas said she was the secretary/PA to the office. Fiona said this wasn't official business. Rosemary supported Fiona. So nobody phoned.

'This meant they were back to square one. The whole idea of the office do, apparently, is that it has to be unanimous. So if two people objected to the Greek place, should they go somewhere else? Douglas said they could always try a club. Fiona sniffed and said she wouldn't be seen dead in that sort of place, full of people in jeans and trainers. Rosemary asked what was wrong with jeans and trainers, just because Fiona didn't have the figure for trousers . . . Then Timothy dropped his bombshell.' Alice paused and gulped for breath.

'Take your time,' said Helen. 'You've all the time in the world.'

'No I haven't. I've only got an hour. Anyway he said he'd already booked a table in the Greek place for the Monday before

Christmas. This coming Monday. And they were all absolutely furious.' Alice stopped.

'Tell me,' said Helen. 'You've told me a lot about your work. What do you do when you're not at work? What do you do at home?'

'Nothing.'

'Nothing at all? What about at weekends?'

'The washing.'

'Why do you do the washing?'

'I can't do it any other time, can I? I'm at work.'

'Have you always relied on repetitive patterns of behaviour for comfort in times of stress?'

'Patterns?' asked Alice.

'Like the washing. Something you do over and over. Playing cards perhaps. Even doing jigsaws.'

'No. Well, I did used to do jigsaws. I wish you hadn't interrupted me. I was telling you about the party. And now my time must be almost up.'

Helen looked at her watch. 'I'm afraid it is. How will you handle your weekend? Have you made plans? It's important for you to have something to look forward to. You must make time for yourself.'

'I'm going to do the washing.'

But when Alice arrived home she found an electricity bill in the hall. She opened it. It was enormous. She couldn't afford to pay it. She couldn't afford to do any more washing.

She would have to plead poverty and pay by instalments. She wrote a cheque for a quarter of the bill, then worked out on the back of the brown envelope how much she'd have left after she received a full month's salary cheque from Holdman and Ray's.

Enough to live on — just. And just enough besides for the purchases she had in mind.

On Saturday she spent a pound on the Tube fare to the West End. She spent £16.99 on a black, button-through lurex top with a scalloped neck and elbow-length sleeves to wear to the office do (with her baggy grey trousers and pink trainers, she decided). She spent three pounds fifty on a 1500-piece jigsaw of a Goya painting of Napoleon on his grey horse (because the horse and Napoleon's red jacket looked exceptionally difficult). She spent a pound on the Tube fare home. She spent twenty-five pence on a black band so she could put her hair up for the party. And she spent Saturday evening working on the jigsaw.

She rose early on Sunday. By lunchtime she had all the edge pieces fitted into place. By 8 p.m. bits of the grey horse were beginning to look like bits of a grey horse. Alice stopped, went into the bedroom, tried the black lurex top with her grey trousers and pink trainers and tried her hair in several different ways. Finally, she decided on a rather complex arrangement with some of it up and some of it down. She set the alarm for half an hour earlier than usual in order to leave time to recreate the look in the morning. She went to bed.

When she arrived at work she found an unusually pale faced Fiona sitting at her usual desk just inside the door. Fiona smiled through red, neatly-painted lips; she wriggled bare shoulders above a plunging, royal-blue taffeta top. She crossed shapely legs in black pumps below a crunchy, puffball skirt. She said, 'Good morning, Alice. Happy Christmas.' The door banged open and Rosemary gusted in on a wave of perfume. She wore a black leather micro mini, a scarlet top to match her scarlet, pointed nails, a dozen gold bracelets. She grinned, flicked her hair back, made her way to her desk, discarded her jacket and pushed the bracelets up her arms. Alice went to her own desk. She passed Timothy: in brown, sharp-creased slacks, a heather-mix sports jacket and an olive-green roll-neck. She slipped into her seat. Henry, at the next desk, said, 'Tuesday, cap T...' then stopped and ran a finger between his reddened neck and the stiff white collar he wore under a shiny, elderly, black suit.

Alice switched on her computer, and defined 'tonight' as 'a special occasion'. Why not? She could always alter it later.

'Well, well, well,' said Douglas, breezing in late as usual. He was wearing baggy beige trousers, a beige jacket with the sleeves pushed up past his elbows and, underneath it, a Hawaiian shirt patterned in the brightest colours. He said, 'Don't we all look smart?'

They looked at one another. They looked at everyone else. They smiled and nodded.

And then the phone rang.

Fiona uncrossed her legs and picked it up, pressing the receiver to her ear, below her carefully arranged hair, above her silver and pearl pendant earring. 'Holdman and Ray's, Dictionaries and Diaries,' she said, then gestured to Timothy. 'It's for you. It's the restaurant.'

Timothy took off his glasses and lifed his extension. 'Yes,' he said. They all looked at him. 'When?' he said. They looked at each other. 'There's no doubt?' he said. They looked down and smoothed the unfamiliar fabric of their party clothes over their knees. 'Not until when?' he said. They looked up again, at him. 'Yes, I quite see that,' he said, his voice dropping an octave. 'And I do appreciate that you're giving us a complete refund. Yes, lunchtime I'll collect it.' He replaced the receiver, lifted his head and announced into the silence, 'Salmonella.'

So they went to the pub around the corner after all. Just like TRAVEL.

the chain pudding

Alice was remembering a scene in a French film. she couldn't remember which film, although she was sure it was a famous film. The scene started with a shot of a pompous-looking businessman sitting at a desk. He said 'cinque', then counted down; when he reached zero the camera moved below the desk to show:

the businessman, who wore no trousers, was being sucked off by a naked woman in red, high-heeled shoes, who

was being buggered by a man, whose

buttocks were being kneaded by a second woman who

was being licked by a man who

was being stroked by the businessman at the desk who

tapped his foot on the floor to help everyone keep time.

And that was what life was like, Alice thought. Things went round and round with a great deal of effort on the part of all concerned and then ended up exactly where they'd started. Only in life, the cycle was less likely to be one of pleasure triggering pleasure, more likely that of pain pursuing pain.

The phone rang.

Alice looked at it. It was on the desk, a couple of inches from her right elbow. After she looked at the phone she looked at the blue biro she held in her left hand, then at the blank pad of A4 wide ruled white paper below it.

The phone rang four times. The answerphone caught it. Alice listened to her voice telling the caller that she was not available, but please leave a message and she would phone back.

Beep! 'Hallo, Joey here,' said a voice. 'I don't know where you've got to,' it complained. 'I've been calling all week. I've left my home number and my number at work. Could you please be sure to ring me this evening, without fail. I'll be expecting your call.' It paused, then added in a rush, 'Bye for now.' The answerphone clicked.

Alice lowered her biro and wrote 'Dear Mike,' then, 'Haven't heard from you, so thought I'd write.' She wouldn't send the letter; but she was going to write it.

Though not like that. She tore the top sheet of paper from the pad, screwed it up and dropped it on the floor. It fell on the answerphone. She looked at the machine. Six calls; five, without the one she'd just had. She bent and clicked the dial to 'Answer Play'. After the beep a voice said, 'Hi. Joey here. Give me a buzz at home later. Or at work tomorrow,' it continued. 'Remember the extension? Six O five seven. That's six (Pause) O (Pause) Five (Pause) Seven. Look forward to seeing you very soon.' The voice stopped, then began again: 'How are you? I've been at work as usual. Nothing special to report. I dare say you've had a more exciting week.' It paused again. 'I did call yesterday and a couple of times before, but your answerphone was on.'

Beep! 'Hi, Joey here. You're always out these days. Must be living it up. Give me a tinkle, when you're free.'

Beep! 'Joey here. I tried to track you down at your publishers, but I couldn't find the Swahili dictionary in W. H. Smith's . . .

Anyway, I'll be at my sister's this evening until about ten and then I'll be home. In case you've lost my number, it's . . .' Alice clicked the dial back to 'Answer Set', picked up her pen and wrote, 'Dear Mike, I am writing to you because . . .' Because what?

The phone started. It stopped after three rings, began again and stopped after two. Alice crossed out the beginning of her letter and glanced at her watch. Time to go. As she stepped into the street and closed the front door she heard the phone begin again.

Two bus rides. A short walk down a rather dark street. Alice rang Melissa's bell and looked at Melissa's front door as she waited. It was painted in wild swoops of primary colours, like a distorted rainbow, and there were symbols around the edges: symbols which, Alice imagined, would have something to do with tarot readings or ley lines or rebirthing or with that therapy thing for which you sat on one cushion, then went and sat on another.

Clara opened the door. 'Melissa's on the phone,' she explained. Alice followed her indoors. Trudi was cross-legged on the floor. Alice mouthed, 'Hi,' and sat on the floor beside her.

Melissa flapped a hand at Alice and said into the mouthpiece, 'Isn't there another way you could come? Some way that you don't have to go down that street?' She paused. 'That's really a pity. But next week we'll be at your place, okay?' She replaced the receiver and turned to face Alice, Clara and Trudi. 'Dorothy can't make it,' she announced. 'It's those men again.'

She went on: 'She did ask me to explain it's not that she's frightened of alcoholics *as* alcoholics — it's that last night she came across one staggering all over the pavement and she was afraid he'd stagger into her and knock her into the road. And *then* she was afraid that if she ended up with a black eye, say, people at her work would think *she* had been drinking. And we know how Dorothy feels about her work.'

'*Does* Dorothy drink?' asked Trudi.

'That would be for her to share.' Melissa sunk onto the floor. 'Did we have a topic for this week?'

'We were going to do issues around make-up,' said Clara. 'But it was Dorothy's idea, so should we without her?'

They all shook their heads.

'What about,' suggested Alice, 'talking about why Dorothy can't get here?'

'Male violence?' asked Melissa.

'Well, sort of,' said Alice, thinking of Joey. Trudi said, 'It's a good topic. But should we make it male oppression stroke harassment? That's wider so we're all bound to have something to share.'

Trudi went first. She told how she put an ad in *loot* for some clothes for sale, size ten, and spent the whole weekend getting calls from men asking whether she had any underwear, condition immaterial. 'Some of them said it was better if it was used.' She paused. 'They meant used recently. A couple of them said they'd pay twenty-five quid per item. A couple of others asked had I anything *like* undies. I mean, what's like undies?'

'What happened?' asked Clara. 'Did you sell the clothes?'

Trudi shook her head. 'I threw them away.'

Melissa said, 'You only have to put your head above the parapet and they're after you.'

Then Melissa went on: 'Mine is maybe more race hatred than male oppression, but it kind of fits so I'd like to share it.' And she told about how she'd been buying petrol for the van and when she went to pay, a man in front of her was arguing with the garage attendant about the price of anti-freeze. Melissa said, quite politely she assured the others, 'Excuse me but could I pay? I'm in a hurry.' And the man stopped arguing and started calling her names.

'What sort of names?' asked Clara.

'Just like that, out of the blue?' asked Alice.

Melissa nodded. 'The garage attendant was Asian and the other man was white and the names he was calling me — 'I'm not going to repeat them — were about white women and black men. Actually,' she added, 'he called me a black cock sucker. Anyway I left the money and went outside and started the van and he followed me and as I drove off he was still shouting. Oh and throwing oil cans at the van.'

'Awful,' said Clara.

'Extraordinary,' said Alice.

'But quite ordinary for *them*,' said Trudi.

Then Alice said a little bit about Joey, about how she'd only been out with him once and then only because she particularly wanted to see *The Handmaid's Tale* and he said he did too. She didn't say too much because her experience with him wasn't really on the same scale as the ones Trudi and Melissa had recounted; he wasn't a complete stranger.

When she finished: 'Asshole,' said Melissa. Clara said, 'I'm glad you told us that because the thing I wanted to say well it's about someone I know too. It's about this guy who kept bringing odd condoms.'

'How odd?' asked Melissa.

'What guy?' asked Trudi.

'Bringing them where?' asked Alice.

'Different makes. Like odd socks. Bringing them when he came to see me.'

'He always brought a packet of three. At first I thought that was really thoughtful. But we didn't always use all of them.'

'When we'd finished he'd, you know, throw the used ones away and then pocket the other one and take it with him. It really got to me.'

Alice: 'What got to you?'

'I don't know. I don't own the man, is the thing . . .' Clara tilted her face again. 'He's a perfect right to have sex with whoever he chooses. But it was the idea of him preparing for it, making provision so soon after, I mean right after. Because, you see, he always brought a full packet of three when he came so he must have used the other one with someone else."

Alice: 'So?'

Clara twisted her hands together. 'I hid the unused one.'

Alice: 'Where?'

'Between the bed and the wall. While he was dressing.'

Alice said, 'Why do they come in packets of three? Are men supposed to do it three times on the trot? Or is it in case you put one on wrong and then another one bursts?' Everyone looked at her. 'Sorry,' said Alice.

Clara went on, 'He kept hunting for the last condom, groping around on the bed and that. But he never thought to look behind it.'

'And?' said Melissa.

Alice said, 'What did you do with all the ones he left behind? You must have lots.'

Clara nodded. 'Left them there, you know? So last week he turned up and we used two of them and afterwards I couldn't find either the packet or the unopened one. But after he left I discovered, not the packet, but the individual casings.'

'And?' said Melissa again.

'One was a Durex nu-form — a white packet with dark-blue and gold lettering and the other was a Durex élite — a green packet with white lettering.'

Alice: 'Well, you can always do the same to him now. With that cache you have under the bed.'

Melissa: 'Surely you won't be seeing him again!'

Clara frowned: 'I don't know. I wouldn't know what to say.'

Alice: 'Maybe you could just come right out and tell him you prefer matched pairs.' She giggled.

Clara giggled too: 'Right after he left and after I'd looked at the casings, I went to the supermarket to buy some tomatoes and I tore a baggie off the roll, but I couldn't get it open, you know? I was standing there rubbing it between my thumbs and forefingers which usually works. Only this time it didn't. And an elderly man shopping with his wife abandoned her and came to help me open the baggie.' She stopped and snorted. 'As though the very fact of being a man would make him more capable of opening a baggie than I was.'

Alice: 'They think they're being helpful. Chivalrous.'

After that the meeting degenerated as — instead of giving each other space to speak and then asking the speaker focused questions — they all began to talk at once, topping one story with another. Alice started to feel uneasy as though — how, she wasn't sure — they might, in a moment, go too far.

But before any question of that, they slowed down and, one after another, yawned, stretching mouths already strained with laughing. Clara leant back against the sofa. Trudi uncrossed her legs and sprawled sideways on her elbow. Alice sat, for a change, on her feet. Melissa rose to hers and said that as it was Christmas she had a present for the group, women! She left the room and returned with three small plastic bowls. 'Friendship cake,' she announced. 'I've photocopied the instructions.' She handed them each a sheet of paper. Alice read on hers:

'Keep in a warm place.

Start as soon as possible.

Do not use a mixer.

Use the same cup each time, and a very large bowl as the mixture increases.

Always cover loosely with a tea towel and leave a gap as it grows.

Day l. Add l½ cups malt extract or honey, a ½ cup (soya) milk and l cup flour. Stir well. Cover with a tea towel.

Day 2. Stir well.

Day 3. Do nothing.

Day 4. Do nothing.

Day 5. As for Day l.

Day 6. Stir well.

Day 7. Do nothing.

Day 8. Do nothing.

Day 9. Do nothing.

Day 10. Stir well. Remove 3 cups of the mixture and give one cup each to three friends. To the small amount left add the following . . .'

Trudi looked up. 'It's a wonderful idea. Like having food together as a group. No, like the loaves and fishes, well symbolic like them, the gift of food,' and rose and kissed Melissa. 'Thank you.'

Clara said, 'It sounds delicious. Pete and I haven't bought any cakes for ages. And we don't even have to *do* anything for a week.'

Alice said, 'It's a chain pudding.'

Melissa laughed. 'But not like chain letters. This is expanding the circle of friendship. In our case sisterhood.'

Alice rode home upstairs on the Number 30 bus with the pudding and the instructions for its growth and distribution in a carrier bag which Melissa had given her between her knees. Then two women in front of her rose and pressed the bell and there was just Alice and a man left, so she went downstairs and finished the rest of her ride there. It was late when she left the 30 bus and there wouldn't be a 43 for ages; she decided to walk. She tucked her keys into one pocket, her purse into another so that if she was mugged they wouldn't find everything at once; and strode off.

The trick was to walk briskly, never loiter, but not so fast that she would draw attention to herself. As long as she kept her head up, eyes fixed on her destination (rounded shoulders were, she couldn't fathom why, tantamount to carrying a placard reading, 'Come and get me'), they never did more than call out after her. She must remember to tell Dorothy that next week.

She arrived home without mishap. She unlocked the door, stepped inside and locked it again. 'Hello,' said Joey loudly from the living room. Alice froze, her hand still on the key. 'I know you've been out all evening,' he went on. 'But I figured you really ought to be home by now. The last Tube must have gone. So where are you?' and Alice realised with a shock of anger that he was on the answerphone, not in the flat. She dropped her carrier bag in the hallway, rushed to her desk and turned the volume on the machine right down so she couldn't hear a word more.

She wasn't tired after that. She ought to tidy up, she hadn't done for ages, but she wouldn't, she would start her letter to Mike again. It would be rather like talking to him, having a late-night chat about the day's doings; like other women, she imagined, did with *their* partners. Not that she had ever done that with Mike.

Should she have? Someone should write a book of the rules of relationships and persuade the Secretary of State to put it on the national curriculum; then everyone would know where she was. The phone rang again, one peal. Even Joey would know.

She should stop pussyfooting, come right out and ask Mike what he was playing at. She settled at her desk and drew, carefully with a ruler, four boxes, one below the other. 'Tick where applicable,' she wrote beneath them. 'You have not been in touch,' she wrote above them, 'because:

(a) you don't want to
(b) you're busy
(c) you need time to yourself
(d) you don't write letters and can't find a phone.'

She added another couple of boxes and wrote:

(e) you don't think there's any point in phoning, you assume it's all right to turn up as and when
(f) in which case you're either a bastard or one of us has misunderstood how we act towards each other.'

She stopped. Once she started trying to figure out why Mike acted the way he did she'd start acting in response to the way she thought he was thinking. And there *was* no way to figure that out.

'(g)' she wrote, 'other.'

In the morning Alice left the letter on the desk, went out and shopped for Christmas. A quarter of chicken, a half-pound of brussels sprouts, a small jar of apple sauce, some bread, milk and a box of cloves; Alice was going to do the festive season properly, no watching the washing over and over, not these days. It was a pity crackers didn't come singly she thought, inspecting a boxful; but how would she pull one with no one at the other end? Don't be a wimp, she told herself. Surely it shouldn't be beyond her to rig up some arrangement with a piece of string?

Christmas morning Alice went out; she walked the grey streets, discovered an open off-licence, went in and bought a bottle of wine. The man behind the counter offered her a little dish of sweets. 'Happy Christmas,' he said. She took one: 'Happy Christmas,' and smiled back. The encounter was so cheering she strolled up the road to the Seven-Eleven, bought a large orange and said, 'Happy Christmas,' to the staff there too.

At home she made her meal. She opened the wine; she tied a piece of string to the living room door handle and tied a cracker to the other end of the string, pulled, but it didn't work. She fetched her mini monkey wrench from the kitchen drawer and fastened that round the nearest end of the cracker. No joy. In the end she unrolled the cracker and pulled the snapping part separately with her own two hands. Same difference. She read her motto, put on her paper hat and watched the Queen, objecting aloud between mouthfuls of chicken to what Her Majesty said. Joey didn't ring. Mike didn't turn up. But she didn't write to him; this was a holiday.

She drank more wine and heckled a Walt Disney film. She ate her chocolate. She left the dirty plate, took the wine and settled in a chair. She watched the edited highlights of the Queen's message, arguing again. At least no one had invaded anyone else this year. Wrong day, she reminded herself; invasions were always on Boxing Day.

On the day after Boxing Day Alice awoke bleared and greedy for real life. She dressed. She emerged from the flat. Pensioners promenading smiled at her. A group of kids on roller skates in baggy trousers and jeans and back-to-front caps around the door of the Seven-Eleven made way for her, grinning. After all, people had been with their families for four days by now, on the trot; they must be bored out of their skulls. Alice, let's face it, was lucky; she had no one to become bored with.

At home again she realised she really ought to tidy up. There were things all over the place, crumpled up letters to Mike on the floor, bits of coloured paper from the crackers, all kinds of junk. She sniffed. At the very least she ought to put out the garbage.

But, what the hell, she had another day yet before she'd be back at work.

She sat down at the desk, threw away her earlier letter to Mike and began again. She wrote: 'Dear Mike, I am writing because . . .' There was a knock at the door.

She stopped writing. Could that be him? she turned the paper over so the writing was face down, went to the door, opened it. Joey stood on the step.

Alice: 'Oh. Hello.'

Joey: 'Hi.'

'What are you doing here?'

'How are you?'

'Fine. Why are you here?'

'Can I come in?'

'Actually, I'm busy.'

'Just for a few minutes. A cup of coffee maybe?'

'Why didn't you phone first?'

'I did phone.'

'I didn't say to come.'

'Yes you did. Well, I said I was. You didn't say not.'

'When didn't I?'

'After my last message. Just before Christmas. And I've brought you a present.'

'Thank you.'

'Can I come in and give it to you?'

'Okay.'

She settled him in the living room in a chair and went to make coffee.

She returned. 'What's the funny smell?' he asked.

'What smell?' said Alice. 'Oh, I haven't put the garbage out.'

He wrinkled his nose. 'It's not exactly like that,' then brightened. 'Here's your present.'

She took it.

'Go on.' He leant forward, hands on knees. 'Open it.'

She did. It was a two-pound box of Cadbury's Milk Tray. 'Thank you.'

'You do like them, don't you? I thought you'd prefer them to Black Magic. Or Cadbury's Roses. Or Newbery Fruits. Or Quality Street.'

Alice nodded, minimally. Joey leant back and crossed one thigh over the other. 'So how *have* you been?' he asked.

'Fine.'

'What did you do over Christmas?'

'Same as most people.'

'What was that?'

'Ate and drank and watched the Queen.'

'I'll bet you did something more exciting. Go on.'

She shook her head.

'You're not making this very easy,' he complained. 'I did ring you. It was costing me a fortune. I had to start making the calls from work.'

'Yes,' said Alice. 'I suppose it is cheaper to visit. Even with the petrol.'

'It wasn't that.' He shook his head. 'I didn't hear from you. I was afraid you'd had an accident.'

'I don't have accidents.'

'You can't say that. You might have. Most of them happen in the home. What *is* that smell?'

'Well, I haven't.' She looked him full in the face for the first time since he arrived. 'I really do have to be getting on.'

'What were you doing?' He looked around the room. His eyes lit on the desk and he announced, with triumph, 'You were writing letters.'

Alice could feel a knot forming between her shoulders. 'Something like that. If you've finished your coffee . . .'

'Thank-you letters for presents? I'll bet you had some nice things. My ex-wife doesn't even run to a card these days.'

Alice rose, seized Joey's half-empty mug from the table, carried it into the kitchen and returned. She stood in the doorway, first on one foot, then on the other.

'Yes, of course, you're busy. I can see that.' Joey rose, too. 'So when are you free?' he went on. 'I thought you might like to catch the next match at Arsenal. I bet you never have!' She backed into the hallway. He followed her. 'It would be a real treat,' he added. 'We could make a day of it.' As long as she kept going she'd soon have him at, then out of, the front door.

But he stopped. 'That smell.' He pointed to the plastic carrier on the floor. 'That's where it's coming from.' He bent and looked inside. He lifted the bag, held it with arms outstretched, showed its contents to Alice.

Inside was the foulest mess she'd seen since she'd been sick after a party, years ago, in a waste paper basket. The mess completely filled the bag, which, now Joey had raised it from the ground, turned out to have a hole in the bottom. Gobs of yellow goo dripped onto the carpet. It even smelt like vomit, rich and spicy.

Joey turned a puzzled face on her. 'What is it?'

'It's a Christmas present,' said Alice.

'What do you mean ? Who gave it to you?'

'For goodness sake stop shoving it under my nose.'

He took a step away from her. A blob of thick yellow slime dropped onto his neatly-creased trousers. 'I can't put it down. It's leaking.'

'You were the one who picked it up.'

'I was worried about it. I was worried about you. That's why I came round.'

The knot between Alice's shoulders unravelled with a suddenness which shook her. 'You've no business worrying about me,' she snapped, the 'b' of 'business' emerging with particularly explosive force. 'I'm perfectly capable of worrying about myself.' She took a step towards him. 'I'm actually very good at worrying about myself. I worry about myself all the time.' She shook a finger. 'I could make a career of worrying about myself. I don't need anyone else to worry about me.' She advanced again but he sidestepped so that he was backing towards the front door, still holding the bag. 'You want someone to worry about,' Alice went on, 'then you worry about yourself. I would if I were you. Yes, if I were you I'd really worry about myself. I mean you really have something to worry about there.'

Joey moved again and a trail of goo dripped after him. 'Get rid of that stuff,' stormed Alice. 'Go on. Take it away and go worry about yourself.' She wrenched open the front door. He stepped out. 'Worry yourself sick. Get yourself into a right state about yourself. But don't come worrying about me. And I hate football.' She slammed the door behind him and looked at the smears on the carpet, then opened the door and shouted down the street, 'It's Friendship Cake,' and retreated inside.

By the time she reached the desk in the living room she was giggling. She looked down at her letter to Mike, picked up the pen, inserted an omission mark between the second and third words, wrote 'not' above the mark, then screwed up the piece of paper and tossed it in the bin.

Now she'd better clear up the rest of the mess.

historical accuracy

'Could you pass me some corpses, please?' Douglas tossed his hair back, ran a freckled hand through it, then returned his attention to the table where the action was.

'Which are those?' Alice inspected the cardboard box of soldiers.

'The ones lying down. With blood on them.' She rummaged, but she couldn't find any. Douglas shrugged, then said: 'I must have lent them to someone. Doesn't matter. It's better to use customised figures, but if there aren't any we improvise with the standard models. Like this.' He tipped a line of soldiers onto their faces. 'Is your coffee all right?'

'Yes thanks. How long does this take roughly?'

Douglas placed two groups of three soldiers on the green surface of the table beside a row of cavalry. 'I thought maybe we could see how far we are by six-ish.' He arranged a clump of trees next to a white plastic house. 'And then perhaps go out for a drink and a Chinese or something?'

'I have to be back early,' said Alice.

'But you did say you wanted to try a complete game?'

'Of course. We could ring up and order a Chinese to have here if we haven't finished. Then I could go straight home after. What are they going to fight with?'

'Sabres or lances for the cavalry — and pistols. Artillery.' Douglas placed a miniature cannon on the battlefield: 'That's the big guns like these — up to twelve pounders. Bayonets. But the main thing for the infantry was the musket; it was called the Brown Bess. See . . .' he pointed to the nearest soldiers, 'I know they're small, yet what you see them carrying are accurate replicas.'

But the Brown Bess was not an accurate weapon, Douglas explained. Yes it could be fired — in the hands of well-trained troops — as often as twice a minute. And yes a musket ball could inflict injury at a distance of as much as 500 yards. But with Brown Bess, a hit at that range was completely accidental. Besides there was so much smoke and so much noise that it was rare for a soldier to know whether his ball had found the right mark. Or care, thought Alice. She would care only whether she were alive. But Douglas insisted they cared about winning.

And winning by the rules, he added, just like in the game they were about to play. 'Did you know,' he asked, 'that during the battle of Waterloo one of Wellington's gunners had Napoleon in range and he asked the Iron Duke for permission to fire and you know what Wellington said?' Alice shook her head. 'He said that generals commanding armies have something better to do than to shoot at each other.' He paused. 'It's a very famous remark.'

Alice said. 'The only thing I knew about the Napoleonic Wars before today was Sweet Polly Oliver. And I'm not even one hundred per cent she's the right period. Oh and I did a jigsaw of Napoleon on his horse. It was called Copenhagen, I think.'

'That was Wellington's. Napoleon's was called Marengo. Sweet Polly who?'

'Oliver. She dressed for a soldier and followed her love. It's a folk song we used to sing as kids. I remembered a couple of verses of it after you first mentioned wargaming in the office. I must say, you do seem to do a lot of homework on all this.'

'Historical accuracy's important. See this?' He held up a mounted soldier on a green-painted base and pointed a stubby finger at it. The horse was in full gallop and the man was screaming through a red-painted open mouth. 'British cavalry. I've done him as the Scots Greys. Trouble with the British, though, is they have a lower value. In the game, I mean.'

'Why's that?'

'Uncontrollable. Once their blood lust was up no one could stop them. At Waterloo they went straight through the enemy and out the other side. Lost 279 out of 300 men. Some of the horses went mad too and bit and tore at the French like crazy.'

'When I was a kid,' said Alice, 'I used to have this terrific game with a little plastic cowboy. The cowboy was galloping on a brown horse with a stiff brown plastic mane streaming out behind. What I used to do was I took a cupful of water and went out into the garden and dug a tiny hole in the dry earth. I'd pour water into it; it wouldn't drain away, the earth was too hard. After that I'd sprinkle dust from the path very carefully on top of the water so you couldn't see the hole was there. The cowboy couldn't either. So he rode straight into it.'

'Why?' Douglas looked at her dubiously.

'So that I could enjoy watching him fall in up to his neck and then struggle in what quickly became thick, black swampy mud. Like Carver Doone. Except I'd have him save himself — he was the sort you can detach from the horse — and then save the horse. All against all the odds. Drama,' she added. 'Going to brink and over it and then back. To see how it feels. That's like this, isn't it?'

'No. This is a re-enactment.'

Alice shut up about the cowboy. 'When you play Waterloo, does the same side always win?' she asked.

'We don't often do it to be honest. It's such a big engagement it would take all weekend at least. Do you realise that there were sixty-seven thousand men under Wellington and seventy-four thousand under Napoleon all told? Even using the ratio of one model for thirty-three men we don't have enough. Usually we don't do historical battles.' He shook his head. 'We make up something smaller-scale.' Then added hurriedly: 'On real terrain, of course. I've just managed to find a series of maps of an area in Greece which is virtually uninhabited. It's ideal.' He continued arranging trees, buildings and several rather realistic rocky outcrops on the table. 'But yes, Napoleon always wins. Logically, he has to.'

'What a lot of people. Thousands and thousands more than Wembley stadium holds. Sorry, but before we pick sides or whatever, where did they all sleep the night before? I want to be able to visualise it properly.'

'On the ground. In the rain. It poured all night the night before. You know the British wore red jackets and white breeches?'

Alice nodded.

'Well when they woke up that Sunday morning the dye had run and they looked as though they were all already covered in blood.' He stopped and looked at her. 'Fact.'

Sunday, Alice thought. 'They woke at dawn,' said Douglas. Five a.m.-ish, thought Alice. 'It was still raining,' said Douglas. Cold wet clothes and cold food, thought Alice. 'Some of them made fires under umbrellas,' said Douglas: as Alice meandered away among the sleepy, red-dyed, rain-soaked men.

At home on a Sunday in high June Polly Oliver would, of course, have been up at this time too; but she would be preparing for a day of very different duties — milking, working in the dairy, mending and going to church. The sun would be bright and would shed some warmth even at this early hour on the little farm in the green heart of Dorset. Not quite enough warmth to prevent her shivering as she closed the kitchen door and ran across the yard with her pail. But the morning was crisp and clean and fresh like her Sunday clothes and like the rest of the day would be.

Not so this day. At every step black mud sucked at her boots (if she would be wearing boots, that is, Alice must ask Douglas). She edged through the crowd around a smouldering, acrid fire. A tattered man held an umbrella over it; a red umbrella, Alice imagined, to match the jackets. One man clapped her roughly on the shoulder. Another tugged her forwards. A third — a giant in brown rags — dragged her off her feet and onto the steaming, trampled ground at the very edge of the smoky flames. 'Unsteady on his legs and blue with cold the lad is,' he said and handed her a biscuit and a mug of tea.

Alice took a sip. It wasn't tea, it was coffee, of course, the coffee Douglas had made. It was tepid by now and made her shiver even in the warm living room, and certainly in the raw, nervous dawn of the eighteenth of June of 1815. She nibbled the biscuit; it was hard and had very little taste. Then they brought round the grog.

'Did they always do that?' Alice demanded.

'Oh yes.' Douglas picked up a couple of dice. 'Standard rations. Have you been listening? We're ready for the first throw.'

'You mean they were always half pissed before they fought? Well I suppose that explains the Scots Greys.'

Douglas said briskly, 'Strictly speaking, you ought to score a six to start; but we haven't got all night you said. I thought this terrain would do for a simplified version of one of the battles in the Peninsular campaign. In summer, of course the scoring gets really complicated if you start having to take snow and stuff into account.'

'Would you mind if we did Waterloo?' asked Alice. 'Or a section of it at the least? I'm really getting into it.'

So they did.

Douglas said best to do the bit near the end when the British had formed into squares and the French cavalry were attacking. He said this was a good set piece and besides it would give Wellington a chance to win as Napoleon had already made a couple of bad mistakes by then. Alice said that was fine by her. Douglas said in that case he'd put the Iron Duke between two squares of troops because Wellington always made a point of being in the thick of the action to rally the men. 'Did Napoleon?' asked Alice and Douglas shook his head.

Polly stood in one of those squares, though not in the front rank nor even the second. 'Could I have Wellington actually inside the square if you're going to charge?' Alice asked hopefully. Douglas nodded and said, 'I'm going to do a morale test on the British. Watch.'

A morale test, Alice learned, is when you throw the dice and then you work out how a group of soldiers will react on the basis of the result and of their position and various other factors. Are they marching up a hill? Through mud? Have nearby regiments suffered casualties? Is the visibility good enough for them to see these casualties? Is there a general to hand to rally the troops? If so, which one? Wellington was the best. There were different scores for all these things and if the group of soldiers turned out to have a morale below a certain level then you had to make them all run away. Douglas called it a rout.

Polly's square, as it contained the high scoring Wellington, did not rout. But the man in front of her threw up his hands, coughed once and tipped onto his face; Polly was jostled forward.

Alice said, 'What would happen if you did a morale test on all of them — the entire 140,000 odd and it turned out they were all ready to run away — could they do that?'

'It's not in the rules.'

'But why not? They must all want to. 140,000 people wouldn't stand around waiting to be killed from choice.'

'They were getting paid for it.' A gleam of annoyance flickered in Douglas's eyes. 'It was their job.'

'That's terrible. Like being in a snuff movie.'

'Look.' Douglas repositioned a couple of fluffy trees with

unnecessary vigour. 'They didn't think of it like that. They thought they were going to be the ones doing the killing. And it's your throw.'

Darkness in the afternoon. A darkness of thick, black, acrid smoke. No enemy to be seen, no friend. Only fumblings in the dark, every man fumbling to fight what he could not see, bodies bumping. Tear cartridge, sprinkle powder, pour explosive, ram in, fire. Unseen missiles pound and whoosh and thump. The smell of burning flesh and cloth, the smell of horse, the smell of sweat and piss and blood. The sound of gurgling in a neighbour's throat, the sound of my own voice, babbling, high-pitched. What is it I am saying so fiercely, over and over? A crash among the many, a rush of air close to and a heavy body thuds onto me hurling me back. I no longer hold my musket or bayonet, I hold something else. Mud or flesh? Grass or hair? I gouge at it with my nails.

The mist clears. Flashes of bright steel. A bloodied mouth breathing warm foul gusts on my cheek. A grey horse writhing. The eyes of a French cuirassier, glazed and hardened with horror as he dies, inches away, on my bayonet. I wrench out the bayonet and struggle to my feet, clutching at the man next to me. He turns and curses me, his face more terrible than the enemy's. And as he curses, he too dies.

'Are you still with it?' Douglas demanded. 'You're Wellington remember. You can't let Napoleon get away with that.'

'Sorry.' Alice shook her head. 'Just out of interest . . . did the soldiers wear boots?'

'Most of them. Why?'

'It would be so very hard for them in all that wet otherwise.'

'It's stopped raining by this time.' Douglas threw the dice. Alice said. 'You know when you read about historical battles they somehow seem quite, well, enticing. Lots of swashbuckling. Acts of derring-do. Exciting in the sense of being elemental, something we don't experience nowadays.'

'I thought you'd enjoy it once we started. That's exactly why I play.'

'But this isn't like that.'

'Well.' Douglas spoke a little huffily. 'You do have to use your imagination.'

the urban jungle

The trick with animals — with cats in the garden, dogs in the street, squirrels in Waterlow Park — is to go down, or in the case of cows or horses up, to their level. That way one was neither bigger, nor smaller, neither aggressor nor victim. It was much the same with people, Alice thought, as she considered what to wear for her outing, it was so easy to become one or the other that we are all a-tingle at the transformation which might any moment take place. And we are never sure which we will become.

She decided she should look like everyone else: which meant jeans and trainers.

Next she considered whether to pack provisions for the day — a Thermos of tea and a sandwich? — then decided if she were hungry she would stop at a café or pub. Who knew where that might lead, that was the wonderful thing about a quest. Think of Arthur's knights, roaming for all those years, seeking, according to the official version, the Holy Grail, but in fact having a series of exciting adventures with dragons and damsels and — for the most part — discovering their destinies en route.

Or think of Milly-Molly-Mandy going blackberrying and finding her path barred by a notice which read 'Trespassers Will Be Prosecuted', then finding a brown rabbit; which was much nicer to discover than buckets and buckets of fruit. So Alice, travelling light, slipped pen and pad into pocket and set off.

It was a lovely day. The sun glinted on the beer cans in the hedge. A soft breeze lifted pages of newsprint and chocolate bar wrappers and hurried them along the street. Alice raised her eyes. Fluffy, white clouds chased each other across a clear, pale sky. Below, grass grew between the paving stones. Purple buddleia nodded, blowsy, from rickety-fenced gardens. There was even, Alice noticed, a tiny blue speedwell flourishing in a gap in the tarmac.

She reached the Holloway Road and set out south, along the route which Dick Whittington followed after he turned. In the middle of the road, on the white line, stood an old pram, its hood towards Highgate. It bulged with rags; several plastic carriers hung from its handles. On the opposite pavement the owner of the junk shop sat sunning himself on one of the sofas he had for sale. Outside the church a drunk lay in a pool of urine, back propped against the wall, one leg bent at the knee, the other stuck out straight, toes upturned.

Alice walked round the pool. The church garden was a mass of shrubs in leaf. She came to the station, a British Rail station with green embankments on either side.

She walked on, avoiding cracked paving stones. They were

easy to spot; the Council had painted broad yellow lines around them. The lines had been there for weeks.

Whole stretches of pavement were cordoned off with red and white tape fluttering between bright orange cones. Inside these enclosures the surface was of fine sand; stacks of square replacement flags stood propped against each other like tombstones in a country graveyard.

Alice circled these obstacles in a series of meanders, like a river. She passed the open space of Whittington Park, sniffed the scent of its freshly-mown grass. The pavement widened; she came to two large trees with benches beneath them, on which a group of winos sat, bottles at their feet, sleeves pushed up their arms, faces raised to the sun. They called out at her. She smiled back, cheerily.

Alice decided to take a bus, perhaps to Highbury, perhaps all the way to the Angel, depending which one turned up first. She joined the crowd at the stop. Beside Alice a woman was talking to herself in a low voice, running one sentence into another as she complained about the infrequency of the 43, the rudeness of some of the drivers when they did turn up and how much, how ever so much shopping she had to carry home. From time to time she repeated a remark more loudly. Alice took a look at her; she was small, elderly, neatly-dressed. So: 'Yes,' Alice agreed, 'I think they are getting worse. But at least it's a fine day.' Two more women nodded. 'Dreadful when it's raining.' 'Weather like this always makes a difference.' They both smiled.

A siren wailed in the distance, then closer. The crowd turned their heads north in the direction of the noise. Alice could see it was a police car, travelling fast. Everyone took a step back from the road. Cars swerved into the kerb.

The police car slid to a halt in front of the crowd. Two

uniformed officers leapt out, leaving the doors swinging, hit the ground running. The woman beside Alice stopped talking; the crowd shrank back. Everyone watched the officers gallop, heavy-footed, to the maroon-coloured car pulled up behind them. They stopped on either side of it and wrenched at the doors. More sirens. A police van arrived; Alice watched its driver park in front of his colleagues' car. Officers climbed from the van. A woman's scream swivelled Alice's head back in the other direction and there, outside the maroon car, her elbow in the grasp of one officer, stood the cause of all this fuss. She was red-faced, but otherwise looked much like anyone else: in pink tracksuit, pink and green trainers. What was she saying? Alice leaned forward. Oh, only that she wanted her cigarettes from the car. She bent in and reappeared with a pack of Benson's and a lighter. The police locked the maroon car, then waved her in the direction of the van. They were taking her away; so it must be something serious.

A 43 arrived and halted beyond the van. The crowd dribbled off the kerb, skirting the incident. Alice was half-way to the bus, when the woman in the tracksuit erupted again, this time into a tantrum worthy of a toddler, face bright, arms flailing, feet stamping, twisting her body in a futile effort to shake free from the police. She flung back her head and screamed, mouth wide, so Alice could see its pink interior. 'Fuck off,' she screamed, 'fuck off, fuck off.' People in front of Alice turned to look over their shoulders. People beside her jostled and craned their necks. People already on the bus peered out of the windows. The driver gazed down on the scene. Two officers pulled the woman into the van and slammed the doors.

The crowd, Alice included, shook themselves and climbed onto the bus. 'Like something out of *The Bill*,' said someone.

'There but for the grace of God,' said someone else. 'The police these days,' said a third, 'they've no call to be that rough.' 'It's the uniforms,' added a fourth. 'Gives them a sense of power, then it's no holds barred.' There were nods all round. 'Nonsense!' cried a dissenting voice, 'she's probably in one of those terrorist cells.' A pause. 'Deserve everything they get.' There were more nods, then a clamour of voices. 'Prison's too good for them.' 'Mrs Thatcher had the right idea.' 'Did you hear that language!' 'No smoke without fire.' 'Ought to bring back capital punishment.' Everyone settled into their seats, smiled at everyone else and the bus set off with quite a party atmosphere on board.

Alice should have made a mental note: 'call = reason. Etymology?' but she just paid her fare and scuttled upstairs.

She wanted to go a long way; she rode to Old Street, then descended into the empty streets.

A warm breeze gusted round tall, silent, glass buildings. Alice walked faster and faster through the desert of the City, fists clenched in pockets. She was thirsty but there was nothing for her to drink here. The shops were shuttered, the streets were empty apart from an occasional pigeon; and there, in the gutter, the stiff corpse of a tabby cat, lips drawn back from bared teeth, blank eyes clouding.

She decided to go even further, to cross the river into the foreign territory of south London.

Alice stood on London Bridge. The sky clouded over, the wind blew across the Thames, carrying the rank smell of wet rubbish. She shivered, then hurried on. The day had turned grey like the sour sludge which lay on either side of the water.

In Borough High Street she was sheltered, but still cold. She would stop for a drink, she decided, then give up and catch the Tube home.

The pub she chose looked okay from the outside, but when she pushed open the half-glass door, a faint smell of stale beer, stale tobacco and disinfectant wrinkled her nostrils. Also the place, though small, was empty; the only bright spot of colour was a flashing computer game. Still, she'd promised herself a drink and she wouldn't stay long. She closed the door behind her, crossed to the bar and bought a half of lager.

Then she couldn't figure where to sit. If she settled on the nearby stool she'd have to talk to the barman, she'd be so close, and she'd heard enough from strangers for today. She carried her lager to the end of the room, discovered an alcove; and there, at a small round table, his bulbous chin and warty nose nodding over a pint of Guinness, sat Henry, Henry from work. He was sideways to her, his glass was half empty, but he showed no sign of drinking what was left. Apart from the slight movement of his head he was quite still.

Alice hovered, feeling caught out.

Henry looked up. Alice was, she realised, staring.

'I was just looking around,' she said.

He nodded at the chair opposite. 'Sit yourself down, girl.' Alice sat.

She drank. The lager was cold, first on her throat, then in her stomach, a nasty feeling. Henry drank too, lifting his straight-sided glass, swallowing, then replacing it with precision on his beer mat. Then, 'Don't live in these parts, do you?' he asked.

She shook her head. 'I was, well, doing some research. Listening to how people use words. The undercurrents of meaning,' she explained. 'What's below the surface.'

'You young people,' Henry's eyes didn't leave his glass. 'Most of you don't know which side your bread's buttered.'

Alice had no idea how to respond to this, but: 'Present company excepted,' Henry went on. 'Working on a Saturday. You know what my motto is?' He raised his head sharply and looked direct into her eyes, his own black ones not in the least old or tired as she had expected, but boot-button bright. 'A fair day's work for a fair day's pay, that's what. No less and . . .' he paused, 'no more.'

'It's as much for my own interest as for Holdman and Ray's,' Alice explained. 'I'll get us another drink, shall I?' He nodded.

As soon as she returned with full glasses, 'No business to be worrying about work out of hours,' he resumed. 'No kiddies, I suppose?' She shook her head.

'Leisure pursuits,' he said. 'Hobbies. Everyone should have a hobby. All work and no play makes Jill etc.'

Alice was about to protest that she had plenty of hobbies, when, 'As for what's under the surface,' Henry continued. 'Eocene clay. Not many people know that.'

'What sort of clay?'

'Eocene. London clay. Which, as it is a very thick formation, proved extremely convenient for the excavation of London's underground railway. The same clay,' he paused and Alice realised, with surprise, that he was showing off, 'is to be found in Ypres, France where, during the First World War, it proved, in the form of mud, a damn sight less convenient for the Allied troops.'

'Geology!' said Alice. 'So that's your hobby. You never mention it at work. Do go on.'

'Work,' said Henry, 'is for work, not chat. Too much of that by a long chalk. What do you want to know?'

'More about London,' said Alice. 'About what's beneath our feet.'

Henry took a long draught of Guinness. 'The London Basin,' he informed her in the level voice he used at work to intone the days, only louder, 'is an artesian basin. When wells were sunk, water gushed to the surface. The fountains in Trafalgar Square were originally fed, entirely naturally, by this means. However, the many pumps raising water have lowered the water table in the basin by more than one hundred feet during the last century.'

'Amazing. It's hard to think of London having any connection with the landscape.'

'London is sinking into the landscape. The Bank of England,' he told her, 'is sinking faster than anywhere else and is expected to be awash in about 5,000 years time.'

Trust Henry to spend his leisure hours in the contemplation of such vast spans of time, Alice thought as she gathered the empty glasses once more and carried them to the bar. Henry was so old himself — older than the hills, as Douglas said, positively Neanderthal — that he seemed ageless. She wondered what else he had up his sleeve. The barman refilled the glasses; she carried them back to the table.

Henry drank. 'Geology,' he said, 'is only a part of my sphere of interest.' Alice nodded. 'And the rest?'

'London,' said Henry, then added as though he were on *Mastermind*, 'The development and evolution of the city from early settlement to the present day.'

'What do you think of it nowadays?' Alice asked, then worried that sounded facetious as though she was implying he was so old he'd seen the entire process with his own eyes.

But, 'Tyrannopolis,' pronounced Henry. 'This, according to

the great town planner Lewis Mumford, is the fifth and penultimate stage in the evolution of a city. In which display and expense become the measurements of culture, moral apathy replaces good living and commerce alternates between expansion and depression.'

'You could be right,' agreed Alice. 'What's the final stage?'

'Nekropolis.' His voice grew louder, sonorous. 'City of the dead. In which war, famine and disease take such a hold that services decline, cultural institutions decay, towns become shells.'

'Oh dear.'

'But,' Henry conceded, in answer to her question, 'it was possible, Mumford believed, for a city to rise again as, for example, Rome.'

On this optimistic note Alice stood up, thanked Henry for all the information, said, 'See you Monday,' and walked down Borough High Street to the station.

The train rattled its way through the eocene clay far below the gravel bed of the Thames. At London Bridge a young man stepped into the carriage and sat opposite Alice. He was late twenties, maybe early thirties, in a dark, conventional, un-Saturdayish suit. His hair was short, neatly-brushed. Nothing much to look at there. Alice looked away.

A hand touched her knee. Alice jumped and was about to scramble out of reach, when the young man said, 'I didn't mean to startle you.' She looked at him again. He was holding an open, brown paper bag, keeping the hand which held it very still, as though frightened of putting a wild creature to flight. 'I only wondered if you would like a satsuma?'

a good idea whose time has come

The cactus was dead. Not only dead, collapsed. It looked obscene: green, shrunken flesh hung over the edge of the pot. Alice carried it, at arms' length, into the garden and left it there, on the patio. And that's when she decided, as she hurried back into the flat, that she must accept that Mike was gone for good.

The cactus, when she brought it, was tough, tall, thick and ever-erect, much like Mike's cock. In fact, she bought it because of the likeness, in their early days together. Must have been a very early day, she reflected sourly, because she bought it because she missed him, yet she was only out shopping and he was at home in the flat.

She never told him why she bought it. With good reason. The cactus was — like most cacti — covered in sharp spines. In this it bore no resemblance at all to Mike's cock, but a good deal, she thought, to his character. Would he, however, appreciate the distinction?

He appreciated the cactus, thought it a fine specimen. Takes one to know one, Alice supposed. He was very particular about how frequently she watered — or more important — didn't water it. 'They hardly need any, they have reserves of moisture,' he explained over and over. Well, this one didn't any more.

Soon after Mike took off Alice decided that had to be that. But she decided with her head which was, she knew from giving up smoking, a very different matter from arriving at a course of action she could stick to. Still, now she had the deflated cactus as a symbol, well, it really was time she put Mike behind her and had sex with someone else. Otherwise, would she ever?

As well as finding a fresh man Alice needed to find a way to publish her dictionary. This meant research, contacting printers, typesetters, learning the business. So one way and another and what with the daily nine to five at Holdman and Ray's she was going to have her work cut out the next few weeks.

She needed more time. Blowed if she was getting up earlier, though. What she should do was manage time better. First run through her daily routine and discover what she could cut, what streamline or what give to someone else to do; then set objectives, attach a realistic deadline to each and — bingo — achieve.

Alice was starting afresh; so she nipped round to the Patels and bought a red exercise book and a brand new black biro. She wrote her name on the front cover and under 'Subject', 'Time Management'. She opened the book. On the inside front cover she wrote, 'Alice Mayer, Garden Flat, 42 Harby Road, London, England, the UK, Europe, the World, the Universe, the Milky Way.' She turned to the back cover and read the multiplication tables, testing herself to see how many correct answers she could remember from school. She read the section on Area and Mensuration; wasn't sure what mensuration meant and looked it up in the *Penguin*. Surely nobody had taught her that word; perhaps it was another of those terms which had changed since metrication?

She opened the book again. What she had been doing for the last ten minutes, she told herself sternly, was exactly the sort of activity the new book was designed to eliminate. On the other hand, now she'd done it, she'd save several minutes every future day in not doing it again . . .

She set to work.

'8 a.m. Get up,' she wrote, then realised that was when the alarm rang, but she always stayed in bed for at least another fifteen minutes. She also realised she sometimes took as much as half an hour to decide what to wear, that she ironed a shirt every morning, wasting precious minutes hovering over the iron waiting for it to heat. 'Iron in bulk on Saturday/Sunday,' she wrote.

What about breakfast? These days she crunched a piece of toast while ironing, which meant she sometimes pressed crumbs and Flora into her blouse which was disgusting but in terms of effective time management could not be faulted. And she never used a plate, so there was no washing up. She remembered, with a choke of laughter, how Sue, when they shared a flat, said her mother used to lay the breakfast before she went to bed — a bowl, a plate, a mug, the box of Special K, the marmalade, the butter dish. Sue used to kid that her mother would save even more time if she ate the breakfast before she went to bed. Which was, it dawned on Alice, a sensible idea. Especially as she wouldn't be ironing in the mornings any more. 'Eat breakfast at night,' she wrote.

No way to cut down on the journey to work; she must make the most of it with reading. Nothing to be done about the time she spent in the office either. Lunch hours she could use for research.

'On arrival home . . .' she wrote. What did she normally do?

She found she had no idea. She pictured herself coming through the front door, wearing her coat, maybe her mac, possibly carrying her umbrella, certainly a bag. Well, she must take off her coat. 'Remove coat,' she wrote. Ah yes. 'Place keys on bookcase so as to be sure, in the morning, where they are.' How long would that take? Thirty seconds, no more; yet the first thing Alice could remember about most weekday evenings was switching on the TV at seven for *Wogan* or, on Tuesdays and Thursdays, for *Channel 4 News*. What on earth did she do for an hour and a half? 'Log early evening activities,' she wrote.

Then, of course, she cooked and ate or she went out. Call that one and a half to two hours, more if she was going to a film.

Then what?

Same problem cropped up after *News at Ten*. Okay, so sometimes she wasn't home, sometimes she watched a late movie, or *Prisoner: Cell Block H* — which evening was that? — sometimes, presumably she wrote cheques for the electricity or the Barclaycard, sometimes she wrote letters, though now, thank goodness, she had stopped writing to Mike; sometimes she talked on the phone though now, thank goodness, Joey had stopped ringing; and sometimes she read. No, she only read in bed. So what did she do all evening? She could allow some time for pottering: watering the plants (she would save time previously spent on the defunct cactus), sticking the washing in, looking in empty envelopes to make sure she hadn't missed anything before she threw them away, taking clothes out of the wardrobe, wondering whether she could alter them and putting them away again — say an hour, no, less, because she never *did* put the clothes away the same evening — but the rest of the time?

Also, did she need to go to bed so early? When *did* she go to bed? Really, she ought to know *that*. She concluded that she went to bed whenever she finished what she was doing. But what *was* she doing? 'Record bedtimes,' she wrote, then went to bed.

The first day of her new regime wasn't typical because she hadn't had a weekend yet in which to do the ironing and besides she'd forgotten to eat breakfast last night, she'd been so busy with the exercise book. It took quite a bit of effort too, to remember to carry it everywhere with her. But nonetheless, at lunchtime, she set off to research bookbinding.

She was sure, she thought, as she swung out of the swing doors of Holdman and Ray's executive entrance, that Henry could have told her all she needed to know. He must have the whole business at his fingertips. But — although he always said 'Good morning' first thing when she sat beside him at her computer — he never ventured another word, not even about geology or what lay beneath London. Once or twice she tried to ask him, but he merely frowned and went on with his litany. Of course, she could track him down in his weekend pub, but how much of her Saturday would that take up, when she ought to be doing the ironing? She strode the length of the building along the main road, then turned down the alley.

From the front Holdman and Ray's looked like any other office building. At the back — Alice had been sent down there a couple of times with messages — was the bookbinding plant. What were those ancient farmhouses called — bothies, was it or longhouses? — in which the cows occupied the ground floor and helped, by their warmth, to heat the living quarters of the humans above.

Well, Holdman and Ray's was like that with the working part on the ground floor.

The factory even looked like a barn. It had huge doors slightly above street level from which the finished products, the dictionaries and the diaries, could be loaded direct onto lorries. Like bales of hay or sacks of grain, thought Alice, then opened the small door cut into the big one and stepped over the threshold.

Other thing about the bookbinding plant was it was full of men. Were any of them likely candidates? She looked about her. Pale, acned youngsters trundled the trolleys, older men worked the machines. They wore sweatshirts or tee-shirts and jeans; one — turned away from her — had a builder's cleavage; another — turned towards her — had a paunch. She shook her head.

All the same it was fun to spend an hour down there, fêted, flattered and flirted with by all of them. She stood alongside a man at one of the guillotines. He had brown, brawny arms; the muscles in them tensed as he worked the equipment; that looked nice. He explained how dangerous the occupation could be. 'Lad I know lost both his thumbs.'

Alice looked at his fingers, hairy and spatulate like Mike's. 'But not you?'

'Oh no. You bet.' He squared up to the guillotine. 'Coming to see us again, are you?'

Alice was late back at her desk and Henry stopped listening to his tape to give her a reproving glance.

All day, whenever a suitable interval occurred, she chronicled, faithfully, the events of her day in the red exercise book.

At 11.30 that evening, after she had eaten breakfast, she sat down to review how she had spent her day.

She discovered there were still vast stretches of time for which she could not account.

In subsequent days, making more careful notes, she found that she spent a great deal of time bumping into things then setting them straight afterwards. Was this normal? Should she enquire about it? 'Dear Marje Proops, My lover left me and ever since I keep colliding with household objects. Is this a common reaction?' Why waste time writing?

She also spent at least a couple of minutes every day rubbing her bruises or searching for elastoplast.

Besides that she spent around half an hour each day deciding what to eat for which meal (including breakfast, now she had time to spare before it). She spent ten minutes each evening flicking channels after *News at Ten*. She spent an average of seven minutes every time she went out, before she went out, checking everything was switched off and that she had keys, purse, comb, cash etc. She spent unquantifiable time rubbing the gap between her eyebrows with one finger; but this didn't count, as she usually did something else — watching TV or reading — at the same time as rubbing.

After Alice wrote all this down she felt quite peculiar, as though someone were watching her every move. She felt incapable of making one, Eventually she looked at her watch, wrote '12.13. Go to bed,' did, but couldn't sleep, which would make a complete mess of her time management if she didn't soon. Should she get up and do something useful? What? She'd ironed every stitch of clothing last weekend. No, she needed her seven hours. She lay staring grimly at the ceiling, occasionally snapping on the light to check the time. At last, shortly after 3.23 a.m., she fell asleep.

In the morning she was

(a) wrecked

(b) late.

So much so she forgot to take her exercise book with her and had to make notes on scraps of paper. However she remembered what was on her schedule for lunchtime: the library.

Once there, she asked the assistant to direct her to the section on printing. He came out from behind the counter. As she followed him, she inspected him. The sleeves of his black sweatshirt were pushed up from his wrists, exposing pale, gingery hairs curling on his forearms; she rather liked that. But when he turned to her to indicate the appropriate shelves, she discovered he had crooked teeth. Also he was far too young. She fixed her attention on the books.

She made her selection, then went into Reference where she read, carefully, the chapters in *The Writers' and Artists' Yearbook* on Self Publishing and Vanity Publishing. All this was all very well, she knew she had a good product, but where was she going to find the money to produce it?

She retraced her steps and asked the assistant about information for small businesses. It turned out there was loads, the library specialised in it. As well as books on cash flow, on retailing, wholesaling, homeworking, marketing, and cold calling there were information packs containing dozens of leaflets from all the major High Street banks. Alice didn't know where to start. She picked out a couple of books and a pack, sat down and skimmed through. She couldn't make head nor tail of all the facts and figures. She stuffed the books back on the shelves, took another two which looked easier, sat, found them just as bad. She slammed them shut.

'Having trouble?'

She looked up. A dark, fortyish man leaning on her table, a man with a squashed nose and wearing a thick navy-blue sweater over a checked shirt. And faded jeans.

'I'm trying to find out how to finance a project,' she explained. 'It's a very good project.'

'Tell me more.' So Alice did.

When she finished. 'What you need,' he judged, 'is to apply to the local EDU. Ideal candidate.'

'EDU?'

'Economic Development Unit of the local council. Exists to get ideas like yours off the ground.'

'Sh,' said a woman on the other side of the table. Alice lowered her voice. 'What would I have to do? And what exactly would they offer?'

The man sat in the chair next to Alice's. 'Under the council's loan guarantee scheme,' he said, his mouth close to her ear, 'you would be able to borrow from the financial institution of your choice.'

'How would I ever pay the interest on a loan?'

He held up his hand, palm towards her. 'Listen. Under the council's start-up incentives for small businesses scheme you would be eligible for a grant to pay the interest on the loan. And by the time the loan falls due for repayment you'll have the money coming in from the sales of your dictionary.'

'What if it's not enough?'

'Then you apply for another grant to cover the continuing interest. Piece of cake. But,' he looked at her out of the corner of his eye in almost the same way Mike used to, 'if you get your distribution right . . . What are you doing about that side of things?'

'Well, I did think Sisterwrite, maybe . . .' 'Sh!' said the woman again.

'Look,' said the man, 'it's really difficult to talk here. Do you have time for a coffee?'

Alice looked at her watch. She didn't. She nodded. For not only was he a mine of information, he was, she was fairly sure, the man with whom she would have sex.

Over espresso in the snack bar next door: 'I don't see why the council would give me money,' Alice said.

'Because you'd be providing local employment.'

'I don't want to employ anyone.'

'You won't have to. You use existing local businesses. The council will see to that. There are a couple of community presses in the area which I'm sure they'd love to support.' He sipped his coffee. 'You see, everyone benefits.'

Alice saw.

'How come you're so up on all this?'

'I chair the committee which gives the grants.' He looked at her, then added quickly, 'Not in this borough, the next one. So there won't be any question of undue influence. But the basic procedures are much the same.'

Then, 'Do you live near here?' he asked.

She shook her head. 'Work. Does it matter?'

'No, after all, you'll be providing local employment. So where *do* you live? Which borough?'

She told him.

'Which area?' he persisted. 'Which *ward*?' She told him. He lived it turned out — what a coincidence — within a mile or so of her flat. 'Practically around the corner,' as he put it. 'If you like,' he went on, 'I could get hold of the application forms for you. Maybe pop round to your place one evening and give you a hand filling them in. As we're neighbours. Oh and I'm Dave, Dave Godwin.' 'Alice,' said Alice. They fixed a date and she left, keeping her fingers crossed for the future, the future both of her dictionary and of her sex life.

She was very late back to work. Henry looked up and grunted.

For the next few days Alice kept an extremely close eye on the time. She even discovered herself setting a limit on how long she spent on each definition — Holdman and Ray's had promoted her to a dictionary of business English for Urdu speakers: which task meshed rather neatly with her own growing vocabulary in this field.

At home, now Alice had dispensed with all her inessential activities, she had ample hours in which to explore the mysteries of business plans and cash flows and accounting systems — with all of which Dave had said she ought to have at least a nodding acquaintance if she was to make the right impression on the council. She even found, now she'd stopped flicking channels after *News at Ten* and stopped looking in on *Prisoner*, that she had time to watch *The City Programme* and the financial bit of the *Channel 4 News*.

And even then she had time on her hands. She sat on the sofa, rubbing the space between her eyebrows with her finger and watching a commercial for the Midland Bank, then thought, 'What about looking the part?' A woman worthy of a loan guarantee and a start-up grant for a small business would not, she was sure, wear streaky pink trainers and grey trousers.

What would she wear? Well, Alice still had that swathe of slippery red fabric in which Mike used to drape her. Plus she had a pattern. Why not make it up?

No time like the present. Alice unearthed her ancient sewing machine, her pins and dressmaking shears. Could she have the whole thing finished by Tuesday, when Dave was coming round? Never knew what you could do till you tried.

She worked at the dress all weekend, ignoring the ironing and failing to make any notes in her exercise book. Monday she went to work in the same clothes she'd worn on Friday. 'Stayed the weekend did we?' asked Douglas with a wink. But by mid-evening the dress was recognisably a dress; and Alice was exhausted. She stopped to rub her eyes and spare a thought for those homeworkers she'd read about. She carried on working into the night.

By Tuesday the dress was — though its hem was held up by large, loopy tacking stitches — a bright little number of a mini. Alice slipped it on over pale, sheer tights and admired herself in the bedroom mirror. Wow!

The doorbell rang. It was Dave, of course. 'Wow!' he repeated, then went on, 'I thought you might like to pop out for a drink before we settle down to business.'

'Love to. Come in. I'll get my coat. I won't be more than thirty seconds.'

The phone rang. Alice leapt to answer it, fearful that if she didn't and after the bleep, the room might fill with Joey's plaintive voice. But it was a man telling her she'd won seven nights for two in Florida. Timeshare, dammit. She should never have answered all those questions in Oxford Street. 'No I can't be at Leicester Square at 10 tomorrow,' she said and replaced the receiver. 'Sorry Dave.'

In the pub they sat as close to each other as Alice had envisaged, possibly closer. She crossed one shiny, smooth knee over the other and enjoyed the unaccustomed feel of tights against newly-shaved legs. She looked — as one did on these occasions — directly into Dave's eyes. His eyes were quite strik-ingly like Mike's, but there any similarity ended; Dave's face was broader, so was his body, he probably had love handles like those men in the films Mike used to bring round. Nevertheless she was growing increasingly warm; lust was like that. Inexplicable.

Over the first round they talked about enterprise initiatives, then about ambush marketing (which Dave said would be a good ploy, given Alice's job).

Over the second round they talked — Alice was making an effort — about Neil Kinnock, about deselection procedures, about the merit of the first-past-the-post system and about the marginalisation of women in politics and the legacy of damage Mrs Thatcher had left to women in the context of the Labour Movement.

Over the third round they didn't bother to talk about any of these things; they talked about themselves and about each other. One way and another, it wasn't until closing time that Alice reminded Dave (or did Dave remind Alice?) about the paperwork in Alice's flat.

Had they eaten? Alice wondered as they left the pub. She didn't remember doing so, though there had been a couple of packets of crisps and some dry roasted peanuts somewhere way back; she could recall crumpling the packets on the table, beside the ashtray. Dave answered her unasked question by stopping at the fish shop and buying two portions of cod; he also procured from somewhere a bottle of wine. Yes, there it was, she could see it, wrapped in green paper, the tip of its neck peeping cheekily out from under his arm.

At Alice's flat they ate and drank. Before they went to bed she checked, out of habit, the time. 'From 11.53 to 12.53,' she said to herself, imprinting the words on her blurred memory for transcription later, 'Sex.' Or perhaps they would take longer?

Alice woke. Light filtering between the curtains. A hammering in her head. A heavy, sleepy body beside her. Relief, in a warm tide, gushed through her. Her back didn't ache, her neck didn't ache. Usually, in those moments between sleep and wakefulness she became aware of pain — a roving pain, located anywhere from the nape of her neck to the small of her back, sometimes even all the way down the outsides of her legs. In her dreams the aches disappeared because she was sitting on the floor, between Mike's legs, watching television, leaning back against him so that she could feel him there behind her, like a wall.

But today she woke and there was no ache and she knew it was all all right.

Mike? She stopped herself, with an effort, from shooting upright. She tilted her face. There on the floor, lay her bright new dress, the tacking stitches in the hem ripped apart from the hurry with which she had shed the garment. There lay Dave's jeans, there his blue sweater, there, arms awry, his brushed cotton checked shirt and there — incontrovertible evidence, given Mike wore M & S striped briefs — his boxer shorts. She lay very still.

He stirred. She feigned sleep. Well, so last night it had all seemed a splendid idea, but last night was last night. She tried to keep her eyes closed, but couldn't. Peeping, she caught a glimpse of tremulous, pimply buttocks, of heavy, short thighs and — yes — of love handles. Hadn't he ever heard of working out? She shuddered. Ugh! He was horrible. What's more she recalled that, just before she fell asleep, he had asked her, quite distinctly, 'Did you come?' How very embarrassing. How very *early* seventies. She closed her eyes and lay still, then thought she'd be better up and out of the bed.

Dave was in the bathroom. She supposed she ought to offer him a Bic. And breakfast. She checked her watch. So late, she'd have to phone in sick. She was sick. She wrapped herself in her towelling robe, worried that she might be better off fully-dressed, and went into the kitchen.

Dave emerged. He came up to her, went to kiss her, but she turned so that his lips fell on the back of her neck. 'Haven't cleaned my teeth yet,' she explained. 'Would you like an egg? Boiled or fried?'

'Fried. Two please.'

She busied herself with the pan. When she next looked up he was standing at the open back door, stretching, inhaling the air of her garden, pleased with himself. And making plans. 'This morning,' he informed her, 'after we've sorted out that paperwork we never did last night,' he looked at her out of the corner of his eyes in a way which was nothing, absolutely nothing, like the way Mike used to, 'I thought we might take a walk. Maybe go up to Waterlow Park, stop for lunch at a pub on the way back.'

'Coffee,' said Alice, handing him a mug. He advanced on her. Alice offered quickly. 'Would you like breakfast outside? It's quite nice enough,' and ushered him onto the patio.

'Lovely,' he agreed, then, 'What's that?' pointing to the flaccid cactus, still drooping over the edges of its pot.

'I don't know. I really don't know,' Alice said fretfully. 'It used to be so healthy. It was for months and months, it flourished. I thought it liked it here. And I didn't do anything wrong. It's not as though I watered it too much. I kept it in an even temperature. I gave it plenty of sunlight. I even repotted it. And gave it a dose of Rootizone.'

'Oh well.' Dave turned away from the pot. 'Perhaps,' he settled himself at the patio table, 'it was just that,' he leaned back awaiting his eggs, 'its time had come.'

why are we waiting?

'We're dying of thirst this end of the table,' announced Milly Moxon. She curled long fingers, red nails gleaming, silver rings glinting, round the stem of her glass and raised the glass in the air.

Victoria said, 'There's a full bottle here,' but she must have spoken too softly because Milly Moxon continued to wave her glass, repeating loudly, 'Dying of thirst. Where's the booze? Dying of thirst.'

Victoria looked at Alice Mayer; surely she'd shush Milly? Instead, she too spoke at the top of her voice: 'Dying of hunger, what's more. Anyone heard of service here? Dying of hunger. Dying of thirst.'

Victoria turned to Bruno Barkworth. 'Not exactly my style,' he admitted. 'But you have to hand it to them.'

Victoria didn't. She never complained. 'It puts people's backs up,' she told Bruno. 'I'm sure the waiters are doing their best. They're probably run off their feet. Besides if we do have to complain, wouldn't it be better coming from you?'

'The token man?' He shook his head. 'Leave it to the women every time. Better chance than I have of attracting a waiter's attention.' He chuckled. 'More's the pity. There's a couple I'd be quite content to attract.'

Victoria stretched her right hand swiftly for the bottle,

topped up her glass, gulped a mouthful. She wished she were at home, she wished she'd eaten lunch, she wished Bruno hadn't said that, she wished Milly Moxon would stop repeating. 'Dying of thirst this end. Dying of thirst.'

She stole a glance at the doorway; suppose Lewis saw Milly Moxon acting like that and thought she, Victoria, was, well, tarred with the same brush? Sweat started from her brow. She hoped the thicker layer of powder would absorb it.

That's what the make-up people hoped when they puffed it on. 'Bit more,' said the man at her right shoulder to the woman at her left. 'Take the shine off the chin, we need to.'

'It's the lights,' Victoria apologised, pointing to the bright, tiny bulbs all around the mirror. 'They're awfully hot.' 'Wait till you're in the studio,' predicted the man, 'cool under this lot by comparison. Another puff, Betty.'

The make-up man was right. In the studio, lights burned down on Victoria with the ferocity of a Caribbean sun; besides which she was face to face with Lewis Black, whose scrutiny, in her book, was sufficient to bring warmth to any woman's face. Lewis smiled, the seductive, white-toothed smile which had made him a celebrity: although he was a linguist by profession. 'Come off it, Victoria,' he said through the smile, 'you can't believe what you write? Not in this day and age.'

She nodded. 'I couldn't write something I didn't feel was true.'

'True?' He tilted his head and the comma of black hair on his wide brow shifted. Victoria's stomach growled; she'd been too nervous all day to eat. Even more nervous now the eyes of the world were on her. And Lewis's eyes. 'Treat to have you with us,' he said. 'First television appearance in how many books? Especially as you yourself — you'll forgive me saying — are

delightful enough to stand in for any one of your heroines.'
Victoria blushed. The audience clapped.

'I'm not a very public person,' she said.

Lewis turned to a different camera; his profile was outlined
against a glare of lights. He went on: 'Tall, dark handsome man
meets lovely but unawakened woman. He makes the first move.
She waits with bated breath. Love triumphs. Is this really a
recipe for the 1990s?' didn't give Victoria a chance to answer
but continued, to camera, 'Ladies and gentlemen. Romantic
novelist Victoria Day. Who is about to join us for . . . *Celebrity
Scrabble!*' A burst of clapping covered Victoria's short walk to
the celebrities' desk.

She watched Milly Moxon take her place beside Lewis and
wished, once again, that she hadn't allowed her agent to
persuade her this would be good publicity. It was a different
kettle of fish for Milly Moxon. In leopard-print catsuit and
stilettos, with flaming shoulder-length hair, red nails, rings,
bracelets, she looked every inch the model she'd once been.
And — judging by the roars of laughter — she was acting every
inch the witty gossip columnist she'd now become. During the
laughter, Milly left Lewis and slipped in beside Victoria.

Lewis introduced Bruno Barkworth, impresario and show
business personality. Finally, he introduced Alice Mayer, 'our
professional lexicographer who this week comes from highly-
respected dictionary publishers Holdman and Ray's and who —
with the help of the dictionaries she has selected — (he waved
at the pile on the desk) — 'will be the final arbiter on whether
the words our panelists come up with can be allowed.'

Alice Mayer, thought Victoria, as she watched her take her
place beside Lewis, was less frightening than Milly Moxon.
Although she too had long hair, it was held back from her face

by a wide pink band and she wore ordinary clothes — a purple brocade jacket over a bright pink shirt and a neat, navy blue skirt. A little odd that her tights were bright pink too, but not that odd, Victoria decided, then realised that the game had begun.

'Head in the clouds, Victoria?' asked Lewis. 'Waiting for Mr Right to appear on the scene?' But he softened the question with the smile which had made the programme so popular with its (largely female) afternoon audience and which turned the palms of Victoria's hands damp as she reached for her plastic letters. She looked at the board; Bruno had come up with 'bosh'. Without much hope she held up 'k' and 'i' to go in front of it. Alice, after consulting a Holdman and Ray's dictionary and shaking her head, said that it was in the *Penguin*. 'It means — as bosh does — nonsense,' she explained, 'but also, of course, the end when you put it on something.' She crossed the floor, took Victoria's letters and slotted them onto the board.

Neither Milly nor Bruno could add another letter to Victoria's word; they had to start again in a different corner. Bruno produced 'po'. Alice nodded; she said it was a Middle English term for a peacock. The audience sniggered. Lewis raised his eyebrows at Victoria. Milly tried 'poss'; Alice hummed and hawed then allowed it as an abbreviation. Lewis smiled at Victoria.

Victoria smiled back. She was still smiling when Lewis reminded her gently, 'Your turn, Victoria. Is it just . . .' he paused, '*poss* that you can make a new word?'

Victoria withdrew her gaze; glared at her letters. She held up an 'l'. Lewis nodded. He had beautiful eyes, dark, like pools. 'Victoria?' he prompted. She seized a letter at random and showed it to the camera.

He frowned sadly. 'We have an "l" and a "q" to add to "poss". I don't think anyone could *possibly* allow that as a word.'

But, 'Oh yes it is,' judged Alice. 'POSSLQ. From the *Feminist Dictionary*, published by Pandora.' She pointed to another volume. 'Person of the Opposite Sex Sharing Living Quarters. Coined during the 1980 US Census.'

Milly protested, 'She couldn't have known it was a word.' Bruno said, 'American usage doesn't count.' But Alice said the *Feminist Dictionary* was published in England and Lewis, his smile widening, said if it was admissible according to this week's lexicographer, then that was that. 'Which puts Victoria at 15 points, Bruno and Milly at 6. Bruno, your round.' But he was looking at Victoria.

Victoria tried to concentrate on the game. Did she want to win? She wanted to please Lewis. She fingered her letters.

Her turn once more. She offered her letters to Alice and to the cameras, but really as gifts to Lewis.

He said, 'A "t" and a "z" to add to "her". Isn't that a car hire firm?' Alice nodded. 'Also a measurement equal to one cycle per second.' 'One up to you, Victoria — well done,' said Lewis.

Victoria glowed. Actually, she sweated. Moisture congealed in her palms, gathered between her breasts, started from her brow. Was it visible — unbecomingly — to Lewis and on screen? The make-up man had said some people did sweat more than others, no help for it; but she was as damp as if she and Lewis were . . . she shivered with heat at the half-thought.

For it was clear — she stole a look at Lewis — that it was very much a thought in his mind. It had been a long time since she'd, well, been with a man, but not so long she couldn't still tell when one of them, well, wanted to. She felt something brush her brow, raised her hand to tuck back a loose hair and discovered a bead of perspiration, crawling through the powder.

Alice was pronouncing judgement again. 'According to Holdman and Ray's,' she said, 'a prefix, therefore not allowed. Meaning: from, down from, away from, out of, beyond etc. But in *my* dictionary,' she added, drawing a large, badly-bound paperback from the heap on the desk, ' "ex" has another meaning . . .' She held the volume up to the camera. 'I'll take this opportunity,' she told it, 'to say a few words about my dictionary.' A spasm of alarm or perhaps a flicker of lust crossed Lewis's face. What would it be like with him? wondered Victoria, slipping into the familiar, delicious dream which always came over her as she wrote the rapturous finale of each book. She forgot, for a moment, that the eyes of the world were on her. She was alone, with Lewis, on the hot sands of the Paradise Island of her last book, basking in the Caribbean sun.

Lewis was speaking, his face straight again. 'In this, the final round,' his white teeth gleamed, 'we begin with Victoria.' Victoria looked hastily at the board.

She held up 'o' and 'n' which were all she had left. Alice nodded: 'Exon. A Yeoman of the Guard or a small section of DNA which carries the genetic information for synthesising proteins. The latter from the *Longman Register of New Words*, 1989.' She seemed, Victoria realised, to have abandoned the definitive tome from Holdman and Ray's altogether.

'And in my book,' Alice went on, 'that is, in my diction-ary . . .' but Lewis cut her short with the announcement that, 'this week romantic novelist Victoria Day takes the stand for *Celebrity Scrabble* Supremo.' He rose and extended his hand.

Afterwards, Victoria remembered little of her sixty seconds in the Celebrity Supremo booth. She remembered only Lewis, very close, as he took the plastic letters from her fingers and placed them on the board.

It turned out, so Milly said later, between gulps of wine, that Victoria had produced gibberish, strings of consonants in which Alice had been able to find no meaning. 'SXRVLT,' said Milly, 'I ask you.' To which Alice responded, 'Ask in that context means "tell".'

So Victoria did not win a holiday for two in Barbados. But she had surely, she thought with a quick glance at the doorway, won Lewis?

Where was he? After the sixty seconds in the booth, he made his concluding remarks to camera. He turned to Victoria, placed a hand on her arm and bent his face to hers. 'Rossi's,' he said. 'The table's booked.' He turned to the others. 'I'll join you, everyone. Have to have a word with the producer.'

Rossi's. Victoria laid her left forearm, the inside of her left forearm which Lewis had touched, on the cool white tablecloth, to the left of her place setting. A waiter poured wine: four flourishes of the wrist, one for each guest; then placed the bottle on the table.

Alice turned to Victoria. 'Thank God that's over. Boiling in there, wasn't it?'

Victoria nodded.

'You still look steamed up. Pity you didn't make the holiday. You came up with some good words though. Kibosh was a cracker.'

'Thank you. It was pure chance.'

Alice said, 'It's probably what I've just put on my job.'

'Oh surely not.'

Alice nodded. 'Bound to get the sack.'

'Oh dear.'

'Can't blame them. I was supposed to be representing Holdman and Ray's. What could I do, though? Chance in a million to publicise my own dictionary.'

'Couldn't you have chosen some less visible way?'

'Contradiction in terms. Publicity has to be seen. No choice but to take the risk.'

'Oh dear,' said Victoria again. Then, rousing herself. 'What exactly is your dictionary? How is it different from other dictionaries? There are only so many words, surely? Or do you make up new ones?'

Alice shook her head. 'Uh-huh. All in the meaning, Take "we". First person plural pronoun, yes?'

Victoria nodded.

'Also indicates relationship. If Lewis said "we" to you, say, he could mean you and he.'

Oh yes. Yes, he could.

'Or he could say it to include all of us. We, the participants in *Celebrity Scrabble*. So it's a bonding/excluding term. It also,' Alice took a sip of wine, 'is used to indicate dominance, the subjugation of one person's opinion, tastes to the unit of the "we", whatever that unit is. As in, "We always like to read the papers in bed on Sundays."'

Do we? Would we?

Victoria blushed.

Alice went on. 'You have to concentrate hard sometimes to catch the nuance of a new meaning. But it's fascinating work.'

'It must be.'

Alice topped up their glasses. 'What about *your* books?'

'What about them?'

'Don't get me wrong. I read a couple and enjoyed them. They read as though you mean what you say.'

'I do.'

'Thing is,' Alice looked around the restaurant, 'wonder where our first course is. Thing is, what about Jackie Collins?'

Victoria shook her head. 'I've never read her.'

'Take Lucky Santangelo. She falls in love like your women. Proper, sweaty stuff.' Victoria hurriedly rubbed the end of her nose with her forefinger. 'She has happy endings. But she keeps going from book to book having sexual adventures. Falling in love again. Also she chooses her men, doesn't wait for them. Plus she runs hotels. Couldn't your women do that?'

Victoria considered. 'I don't think so.' She shook her head. 'I think my books are wish fulfilment.'

'Nothing wrong with that,' chipped in Milly, loudly from the other end of the table. 'We're all in the running for a good bonk.' Victoria's eyes strayed to Lewis's empty chair. Milly said, 'Yeah and we all agree he'd do nicely. Knows it himself. Thinks he's God's gift.'

Victoria grew even hotter.

Milly launched into stories of other men she'd come across who thought they were God's gift. The stories were anatomically detailed and both Alice and Bruno seemed to find them very funny. Victoria tried to laugh too, but only managed a small, choked sound. None of the others noticed.

Victoria thought: what should she reply when Lewis asked? What exactly would he ask on this, their first evening? She imagined the two of them together. In her imagining Lewis had unfastened heavy gold cufflinks and rolled up the white, silk sleeves of his shirt. He leant towards her. What next? She shook her head. Of course, she should say no.

'Anyway,' Milly was saying, shouting rather, 'there I was on the Tube in the rush hour and we're all pressed up against each other.'

'Yes?' said Alice.

'Go on,' said Bruno.

'So this guy's squeezed against me and I can feel what's happening. I can't move an inch, but this guy manages to move a whole lot more than that. I'm trying to read the *Guardian* media section, right? Visualise it. With his dick digging into my coccyx.' Milly stopped, took a gulp of red wine, demanded, 'Where the fuck are the waiters in this place?' and continued. 'So we get to Oxford Street. He's still doing his business in the small of my back. At Oxford Street there's a lot of people getting off and on, so I figure here's my chance to be heard. I take a deep breath,' Milly took one, 'and I tell him at the top of my voice,' she told them at the top of her voice. 'Get your fucking penis off my back.'

The restaurant fell silent. A waiter hurried over, looked at Milly and Alice, then asked Victoria if there was anything she required. 'Fucking well is,' said Milly. 'We want our dinner. It's all paid for. Check your bookings under Lewis Black. We're supposed to be celebrities, for God's sake.' The waiter hurried off. He disappeared behind a swinging, green baize door.

He reappeared with several plates of steaming food; and carried them to a group of people at a table on the far side of the room.

Then: 'We're dying of thirst this end of the table,' said Milly Moxon. Over and over.

Victoria's stomach grumbled. She coughed to cover the sound, but, 'You and me both,' said Bruno. There was still no sign of their food. Perhaps Milly Moxon would calm down if only they gave her something to eat? Victoria looked at the bright spots of colour in Milly's cheeks and had her doubts. She herself was extremely hungry. And slightly drunk.

Did she really want to sleep with Lewis? she wondered. If so, was it *wise*? One heard so much these days about Aids, but it would be embarrassing to ask about precautions. She shook her head. No, of course, Lewis would take care of all that.

A waiter passed the table. Milly Moxon shot out a hand and seized him by the sleeve. 'If you won't bring us food, then bring us the manager.' The waiter scuttled away.

'This'll be worth watching,' said Bruno. And Victoria, though still alarmed, awaited developments with a good deal of awe for Milly's daring.

According to the manager, when he arrived, the explanation was perfectly simple. 'The meal was ordered for when Mr Black arrives. He said he might be a little late, madam, and asked us to serve wine while you waited.'

'Sod Mr Black,' said Milly.

'Perhaps we should wait,' suggested Victoria.

'Wait, nothing,' said Alice. 'Where *is* Lewis Black?'

'We are a trifle hungry,' added Bruno.

The manager fluttered his hands, then agreed to send their starters. 'And more wine,' shouted Milly at his retreating back.

'Don't you think we could be a bit quieter now?' Victoria begged.

The waiter returned. He set a bottle of wine and a basket of bread rolls on the table and a tall glass dish in front of each of them. ' "We",' said Alice, 'in that sentence, is used as an indicator of the speaker's willingness to share the blame for another's actions if the other, in return, stops taking those actions.'

Victoria crumbled a bread roll.

She picked up her fork.

'I can't eat this!' shrieked Milly Moxon. She poked at her prawn cocktail with a soup spoon. 'I told them when I agreed to do the show that I wanted vegetarian.'

Victoria slipped a prawn into her mouth. 'I do too,' agreed Alice. 'Though I forgot to mention it myself.' The prawn was tasteless. Victoria tried a scrap of lettuce. 'You don't have to eat that,' Alice told her. She picked up her dish and strode off through the swing door. Victoria heard raised voices. What would happen next? Alice returned empty-handed.

'Well?' demanded Milly Moxon.

'Coming up.' Alice slipped into her chair. Sure enough the waiter appeared and set avocado vinaigrette in front of Alice and Milly. 'Four,' said Alice. 'Not two.' She turned to Victoria and Bruno. 'You want this as well, don't you?'

'It does look nicer,' ventured Victoria.

'But they were ordered,' said the waiter. 'The prawn cocktails.' Victoria was about to agree and to mention that as she had taken a bite or two of hers she should, she supposed, finish it; but 'We're the customers,' said Alice. 'We choose, not you.' He took the prawns away.

The avocado proved delicious. But instead of calming Milly it seemed to fuel her grievance. She demanded more bread. The waiter brought a fresh basketful. Victoria had to admit, reluctantly, that Milly and Alice between them, outrageous though their behaviour was, were having an effect. On the other hand it was all so unnecessary and so unpleasant for the waiters and the other diners. If only Bruno would speak up. If only Lewis were here, there would be no problem. If there was, Lewis would surely solve it. At once.

But Lewis did not arrive. Nor did the main course.

'I really am,' Victoria admitted helplessly to Bruno, 'rather hungry.'

'Well you're the biggest name.'

'What?'

'Best known. You could always toss it into the fray. Might work wonders.'

But Victoria's name meant palm-fringed beaches and tall, dark men (where *was* Lewis?) and feminine women who waited for him to make the first move; not viragos bawling at waiters.

Milly and Alice were both bawling. The manager reappeared and made soothing noises. He beckoned waiters with more wine. To Victoria's surprise Milly and Alice subsided. Were they worn out from the arguments? Were they too drunk to carry on? Had they simply given up?

Victoria had always cried easily. She cried whilst writing the final scene of each of her novels. She cried when she came across, in a magazine, a picture of an especially pretty baby or an adorable kitten. She cried in movies. She cried when — on the news — she saw reports of people starving or unable to obtain proper medical treatment. Usually she allowed herself to cry, she saw it as an essential part of her sensitivity, the emotional vulnerability which enabled her, in her writing, to penetrate to the heart of romantic love.

But now, as she felt tears pricking her eyes, she was sure that the one thing she didn't want in the whole world was to break down.

Nor to see Milly and Alice defeated, to see such bravery — however foolhardy, however vulgar — crushed into compliance. So instead of weeping, she scraped back her chair and rose to her feet.

'Miss Day,' murmured a voice at her elbow. 'Miss Day, I

recognised you from the photo on your book jackets. My wife loves your books and I wondered . . .'

She ignored him and rounded on the manager. 'Do you know who we are?' she demanded, far too loudly. He shook his head. 'Do you know who I am?' Another negative. She faced him, hands on hips, and announced, so the whole restaurant could hear. 'I am Victoria Day. And I am hungry.'

She had no idea whether he knew who she was. She did know, all of a sudden, that it was possible to act like this and to provoke a reaction; that she was getting one hell of a kick out of it; that a crowd was forming, holding paper napkins and scraps of paper for her to autograph; that a flashbulb was popping near the restaurant door.

'Victoria!' It was Lewis's voice. 'Whatever is the matter?' More flashes.

Alice and Milly revived and turned on Lewis; but Victoria's voice was the loudest. 'Where the hell have you been?'

'Meeting the photographer. He rang from the Press Association. They want pictures of you all. For the nationals. Victoria, please calm down.'

But she held the floor as she never had. 'Do you realise how long we've been waiting?'

'How long what?' He looked at the table with the barely-touched place settings. 'Surely you didn't wait for me? Why?'

'Because you ordered the meal for when you arrived, that's why.'

'My God.' He struck his brow with the flat of his hand. 'I completely forgot.'

'They didn't. You ordered it for when you arrived. As though you were the celebrity. You're not the celebrity. I am.' She paused, then gestured at Milly and Alice and Bruno, 'We are,' spun round to face the manager. 'Now get us something to eat.'

'What,' asked Bruno, grinning, 'will your fans make of that?'

'Whatever,' Victoria dismissed with a wave of her hand the disturbance she'd created, subsided into her seat, borrowed a pen and wrote 'Love from Victoria Day' on one of the napkins.

Later, after she finished signing autographs, after the food arrived, after the urgency of the first few mouthfuls was over, she discovered the photographer was gone and Lewis was sitting opposite her, hang-dog.

'Victoria,' he began. 'I really am most terribly sorry. I had no idea.' When she didn't respond he pressed on: 'But now I'm here and that's all cleared up and we've given you something to eat.' He flashed his white teeth. 'I'd no idea you'd be so forceful. Positively fiery.'

Victoria wasn't fiery. She wasn't even hot. She was ice cool.

'It wasn't only the photographer who delayed me,' Lewis added. 'Someone from Holdman and Ray's phoned to complain about my letting Alice Mayer go on about her own dictionary like that.' He lowered his voice. 'Extraordinary woman. Not to say either Milly Moxon or Bruno Barkworth are either of them exactly what you'd call normal.' He leant back and sighed, 'What a night!' then leant forward across the table. 'But as soon as the others have finished their meal we can make plans. You and I can make plans. Where would you like to go on to? I thought maybe Groucho's. You can't have been there. And I am a member.'

Victoria turned away, leaned her elbows on the table and asked Alice, 'Shall we go somewhere later?'

It was Bruno who nodded. 'Would Paradise be all right?'

Before Victoria could ask what he meant — 'I'm game,' said Milly, 'If they let women in.'

Bruno nodded again. 'But Lewis won't want to,' Alice pointed out.

'Tough,' said Victoria. 'Alice, which of the Lucky Santangelo books should I read first?'

opportunity has knocked

Drivers of black cabs are drivers of black cabs; minicab drivers are poets or playwrights or resting actors or — like Bert — they are stand-up comics. A few of them are also — and also like Bert — failed apprentice jewellers, failed plumbers' mates, failed market traders and failed husbands.

'Oh yes,' Bert would assure his late-night passengers, glancing at them in his mirror as they lolled, drunk, against the torn upholstery, 'I've had my ups and downs. But right now I'm on an up. Yes, you could certainly say, I'm on an up.'

He was driving north at the time, climbing the steep hill of the Archway Road. 'Funny old thing, life,' he confided. 'But you have to laugh.' He passed under suicide bridge. 'Could have been me up there,' he went on, 'few years ago. Few months even. But now,' he puffed out his chest, 'now I'm waiting to hear when I'll be hitting the heights.'

Or another night, as he swung down the long slope of Haverstock Hill; 'Way I see it,' he said, 'life is like a roller coaster. One minute you're racing up, next minute you're plunging down. But look at it like this,' he paused, 'once you're at the bottom, only way out is up.'

'What I tell people,' he went on, 'is think about the Irishman who tore along the dotted line.' He glanced in the mirror. 'Not Irish are you? Never knowingly cause offence. Haven't heard that one? Who am I to refuse? Always raises a chuckle.'

Next day Bert, working an early shift, had a lunchtime pick-up from Heathrow. Good news that, the firm usually stuck to drivers whose cars were in better nick. Plus he liked the long runs, gave him a chance to establish a rapport with his passengers. Beat him, though, why people didn't pick up a cab at the terminal. More money than sense, some of them. Still, his not to reason why. He set off.

Sure enough, his fare looked like he had a damn sight more lining in his pockets than most. 'Nice suit,' Bert thought as he stowed a soft brown leather case in the boot, 'Ray-Ban's must have cost a packet.' Something familiar about him, wasn't there? Bert never forgot a face, prided himself on that. He shook his head; probably seen him on the box, had that happen before. He slipped behind the wheel.

As soon as they were on the road: 'Been anywhere nice?' he asked. 'Somewhere in the sun by the look of you.'

'Greece,' said the passenger.

'Funny you should mention that,' said Bert. 'Mate of mine at school, he was Greek. Real name Georgios, but we called him Greg. Cheeky devil. Not that I was any better. Bigger than him, though. I have always,' he added proudly, 'been big.'

'Gives you an edge,' Bert went on, 'being big does. Mind you not that Georgios, Greg, that is, did badly for himself, not by a long chalk. That's what counts, you agree with me there?'

'I can't hear you nodding,' quipped Bert. They were on the

motorway now. 'Just one of my little jokes.' He drew out to overtake a Gentle Ghost van. 'Greg and I we don't keep in touch, wouldn't put it like that. But, you know how it is with mates, every few years we bump into each other.'

'How long to the centre of London?' said the passenger.

'Funny you should ask that,' said Bert. 'I was just about to say it should be a clear run till we hit the Brompton Road. This mate of mine,' he went on, 'you have to hand it to him.' He settled into a steady speed in the middle lane. 'Never did a stroke at school. Said there were other ways of getting on in life. Right, as it turns out. See that?' he pointed to a Rover in the outside lane, 'driving one of those last time we met. Selling them, see. At the top end of the market, mind you. Rollers, Jags, you name it.'

'Few years back, that was now,' Bert continued. 'Probably wouldn't recognise him if I came across him in the street. But always had the knack of being in the right place at the right time, he did. Ran across him at the height of the property boom: an estate agent in Crouch End. Up and coming neighbourhood, trust Greg.' He sighed. 'Wish I had his luck, landlady's cutting up rough about the rehearsals, says she can hear every word through the wall. Could be joining the army of the homeless come next week. Still,' he smiled, 'Yours truly can't complain. Not with my prospects.'

'What prospects?' said the passenger. 'What rehearsals? What do you mean?'

'That's asking. Thought for a moment you'd dropped off back there. But seriously. Opportunity has knocked. This month a single slot. Next month a regular billing. And next year, well, sky's the limit. No question of whether, s'just a matter of when.'

'At what? What are you on about? What do you do?'

'Comedian. There. Knew you'd be impressed. Mind if I

smoke?' He watched, in the mirror, the passenger shake his head, Ray-Ban's gleaming. He groped in his jacket for his Red Bands. They'd slipped through the torn lining again. He struggled, then managed to extricate the packet. Cigar lighter didn't work these days; he struck a match, the car veering a little as he did so. 'You know,' he confided, 'when me and Greg were kids we pinched a thing — one of those projects kids do — off a girl at school and got a gold star for it. Call me a fool but ever since I've wanted to earn my own gold star. In a manner of speaking. And now, well!' He exhaled a cloud of smoke. 'The other memory I have of Greg,' he went on, 'we used to go to the fair on the Heath on Bank Holiday. Shooting range, hoop-la, dodgems. And roller coasters. Greg in one car, me in another. Seemed to me every time I saw him he was on the way up, I was going down. Like life in a way. But if he could see me now!'

'I remember the roller coaster on the Heath too,' said the passenger. 'And,' he went on slowly, 'I remember Alice Mayer's word wall. Like it was yesterday.'

Bert jumped so suddenly, the car swerved and the driver of a BAA bus gave an angry blast on his horn. 'Pull the other one,' said Bert, straightening the wheel. Then, quickly. 'Just joshing. Of course I knew all along.'

For a moment or two he drove in silence; up the Chiswick flyover, then down the other side. He grinned broadly. 'Had you fooled with that guff about how I admired you, didn't I? Joke's on you, Greg.' He went to slap his thigh, realised he was still holding his Red Band and raised it to his lips instead. 'Funniest thing since the one about the feminist who wanted to cross the road. You pretending you didn't know me from Adam. Me kidding you along.' He inhaled on the stub so hard his lips felt burnt. 'So what since the motors?'

'Security.'

'Window locks? Burglar alarms? Pretty good market I dare say, crime the way it is. I always said you had your finger on the pulse. Not that I can't blow my own trumpet.'

'True. Real success story. But not the domestic market. Something bigger.'

'Not,' said Bert, awed, 'defence? Not *armaments*?'

Greg laughed. 'Wrong again. But upmarket. Very upmarket. Rubbing shoulders with the rich and famous.'

Bert was silent again. They reached Knightsbridge. Then: 'Have you met Princess Di?' he asked.

He squinted in his mirror. Greg had removed the Ray-Ban's and was leaning back, smiling. 'No. Jerry Hall I have, though. And Brian May and Anita Dobson.'

At Hyde Park Corner a group of tall, shiny horses with riders in spotless white breeches, black jackets and black velvet caps clattered out in front of them. The leading rider held up his hand; Bert stopped to let the group pass. 'Bet you can afford that these days for your, what was her name, Fiona? One for the horses, wasn't she? Regular county type.'

Greg cleared his throat. 'Fiona's past history. How's Janet?'

'Actually.' Bert watched the riders reach the sand of Rotten Row and canter off. He slipped in the clutch and started up Park Lane. 'Janet left me. Couple of years ago now.'

'Nothing to write home about,' he added quickly. 'Dear Mum, my wife says I should get a regular job, nothing like that. You have to laugh.' He did so, an odd, chortling noise. 'Where after Marble Arch?'

Greg directed him along Oxford Street, High Holborn, then towards the City. 'Flat in the Barbican, eh? said Bert. 'Very nice.'

'Getting back to your work,' said Bert, 'what about the comics? Ever meet them? Jasper Carrot? Ben Elton? Hale and Pace? Great double act, that.'

'I have come across them,' said Greg. They went on talking celebrities.

Twenty minutes later Bert drew up, at Greg's direction, in a street behind Brick Lane. 'Here?'

Greg nodded. 'Only temporary quarters. How much do I owe you?'

Bert told him. They both climbed out. The spicy smell of curry hit Bert's nostrils. He opened the boot and handed Greg the brown leather case.

Greg peeled several notes from a thick wad. 'Want to come in?'

Bert counted the notes; he'd earned his whack for the day. He nodded.

Greg led the way to a shopfront. There was a scrawled notice in the window. 'Best prices paid,' Bert read. 'No job too small.' Greg unlocked the door beside the shopfront; Bert followed him upstairs. They entered a bleak, cold room, with peeling paper, black smudges of rot on the walls, a formica-topped table, a moth-eaten rug, a collapsing sofa. 'Make yourself at home,' Greg invited and went through an open door into a dingy kitchenette.

Bert lowered himself gingerly onto the edge of the sofa. He clasped his hands between his thighs and looked at them. A great sadness descended and, carrying him with it, plunged to depths he had never before imagined. So Greg had come down in the world.

He should leave, he thought. But he made no move, only twisted his hands together so that the fleshy pads at the root of each thumb turned white with the force of his own grasp.

Greg returned, whistling, carrying a bottle of Jameson's and two glasses. He poured generous measures and handed one to Bert. 'Get this down you,' he advised. 'It might never happen.'

Bert drank, then said out of habit, 'Funny thing you should mention that . . .'

'Because it has, right?' Greg tugged at the sharp crease on one leg of his immaculate trousers and sat on a sagging chair. 'Nowhere to hang your hat?'

'So,' he went on, 'you said you had landlady problems.' He downed a large mouthful of whiskey. 'How does sharing this place grab you? Least I can offer seeing we're old mates.'

Bert's eyes slid around the dilapidated room; he wished they hadn't.

'Not palatial, I grant you,' Greg admitted. 'But with my lifestyle I only come here to crash. No point wasting money on a place I hardly use.'

Bert roused himself. 'Rent it, do you?'

Greg shook his head. 'Own. And the commercial premises below. Market collapsed just as I was about to offload. Little gold mine, though, for someone with an eye for these things. Development potential. Worth my hanging on for the right price.'

Bert looked around the room again. So the chairs were rickety, so the formica-topped table wobbled. But over one chair, he noticed, was draped an expensive — Armani probably — suit, over another a Pringle sweater. And Greg was, besides, an owner occupier. Yes, Greg had fallen on his feet again.

'Cheap to heat too,' Greg crossed the threadbare carpet and lit the gas fire beneath the chipped mantel.

He was right. Bert could feel the warmth straight away. He spread his hands.

'Another thing,' said Greg. 'How come you're on the cabs, performer with your future? Do much better where I am. Plus a bit of cachet for us, seeing your name's going to be in lights.'

'Us?' said Bert. 'What exactly is it you do?'

Which is how it came about that Bert became Greg's lodger and that Bert joined Greg as a bouncer on the door of the Nightmare Club. Greg, so he told Bert, had a stake in the management, although Bert saw no evidence of this. But — be fair! — neither did Bert explain that what he was waiting to hear about was a one-minute slot on *Opportunity Knocks*.

Still, no skin off anyone's nose. Because every evening now Bert rubbed shoulders with the rich and famous (he never forgot their faces): and turned the not so rich or so famous brusquely away.

One Wednesday — which was always Paradise night at the Nightmare — Bert spotted, in the queue, a woman who looked like Alice Mayer. He pointed her out to Greg. 'Could be,' Greg nodded. But as Alice Mayer wasn't famous and as she was with a small woman whom neither of them recognised and with Bruno Barkworth and Milly Moxon who were only minor celebrities, they didn't bother to speak to her. But, seeing as she *was* with them, they did let her in.

from the wrong angle

When Sue returned from Russia she decided to murder her mother.

It was the first time such a thought crossed her mind.

She didn't think it while she was *in* Russia: not on that bright Sunday afternoon in a main street in Minsk when the gypsy seized her arm and dragged her towards a group of dark men in a dark doorway. She didn't think it when she was unable to shake free. She didn't think it when his grip bit hard into her flesh. She didn't even think it when she roared a protest and not one of the scores of neatly-dressed people promenading past moved a step in her direction. No, it wasn't until the end of the trip and she was safely back and behind the morticed front door of her London flat that the thought occurred to her: occurred to her because — now she had time to think about it — the incident was further evidence that her mother might be right.

When Sue was small her mother was always right: about everything. These days, Sue reflected, as she abandoned the idea of unpacking and opened a Duty Free Bells instead, no one used the words 'right' and 'wrong' as absolutes on the scale of morality. These days the terms were much more a matter of style. She wandered into the living room, poured the whisky into a glass, settled herself on the sofa and unzipped her hand luggage.

She tumbled out onto the floor: two Dorothy L. Sayers, a Ruth Rendell, a Patricia Highsmith and a clutch of postcards. She picked up the postcards and inspected them: improbably coloured minarets in Moscow, snow covered domes, a few close-ups of ceramics and religious icons. These days you said, 'You're looking at that icon from the wrong angle,' but you didn't say, not with finality, of an action or an impulse, 'That's wrong.'

Sue topped up her glass. She turned the postcard over and wrote on the back of it, 'Ways of Murdering My Mother,' then pushed the card aside and pulled out a notebook. As her mother always said, 'If a thing's worth doing, it's worth doing well.'

'Method,' she wrote. She underlined the word, then paused.

'Poison,' she wrote.

Then: 'Stabbing.'

'Decapitation.'

'Shock?'

The first could be done with mushrooms maybe. Sue knew the difference between an amanita phalloides and a field mushroom, but her mother didn't. If this were fiction it would be easy to slip one into a stew. But if she did that could she manage to avoid it herself? Sue's mother was always so insistent about Sue eating up.

For the second method she would need a knife. Her bread knife? One of Ruth Rendell's characters had used one, Sue recalled. But the woman concerned had been demented by panic, otherwise surely a serrated blade would be too ghastly for anyone to consider. Sue shivered. A Sabatier? No, Lawrence had taken those. Typical of Lawrence.

She sucked her pen. 'Decapitation?' then shook her head. Even Agatha Christie, in the most far-fetched of her middle eastern mysteries, had never gone so far as that. Shock might be better; but Sue'd already done everything which could possibly shock her mother.

She sighed. She had started to shock her mother before she could remember; in fact the earliest thing she could remember was her mother standing over her, shaking a finger and saying, 'Oh no dear, we don't do that.'

But Sue did. She read in poor light ('You'll damage your eyesight'); she stayed indoors to read ('You'll ruin your complexion'); she wore the same ancient sweater weekend after weekend ('You'll become a slut'); she let her fringe hang over her eyes ('You'll end up with a squint'); she slumped sideways on chairs or sat cross-legged on the floor with her head bent over a book ('You'll develop a dowager's hump').

Later, Sue wore orange lipstick and sparkly green eyeshadow ('You'll look cheap'). She smoked ('All right, if you *must*. But certainly not in the street'). She went to parties and came home drunk ('You'll regret it when people talk'). And after the parties, on the way home, in the inky blackness of the allotments between the rows of pungent cabbages, she did things with the boys from the sixth form for which, had her mother known of them, she would have condemned Sue to the wholesale disrespect of the entire male population of the British Isles.

But Sue grew up without needing glasses. Her complexion remained pink and white. Baggy sweaters became fashionable — as did droopy fringes. Everyone sat on the floor; everyone came home drunk; and everyone made out. As if that wasn't proof enough, Sue achieved several A levels, ('You don't want to turn into a bluestocking, do you?') then a good degree ('Men don't like clever women, but I suppose you think you know best') and then a job as a copywriter ('You're not going to end up one of those *high-powered* women, surely?'). She rented a flat with Alice ('It won't do you any good to be seen with that girl. Too flighty') then bought a flat with Lawrence ('A man with a *beard*? He'll never settle. And I suppose you're footing the bills?'). Recently Sue had taken to travelling — on her own and with immense enjoyment ('I worry about you wandering around by yourself in foreign countries. You don't seem to think of the dangers. A single woman is always vulnerable. I only hope you realise before it's too late').

Sue didn't. Because all the evidence suggested that her mother was wrong; in the sense, that is, of being incorrect.

But maybe not now? Sue returned to her list and wrote 'Opportunity' wi.h such ferocity that the lead of the pencil snapped. She rummaged in her bag and found a biro. How about next weekend? She could pop home — she hadn't been home for ages — and her mother would welcome her as ever.

She nodded twice, reached for the whisky bottle, then realised she was half-drunk and that she had to go to work tomorrow. She went to bed.

For the next few days Sue worked late each evening and arrived home too tired to do anything other than eat and drop into a deep sleep. And then she woke and it was Saturday.

The sun was shining. She threw off the duvet and scrambled into her favourite, soft black leather trousers and a black sweatshirt. In the kitchen she drank a single cup of coffee. She was going shopping for food and she always did this on an empty stomach; it made the pleasure keener.

In Safeway's she lingered at the delicatessen counter, inspecting the pâtés and cheeses and salamis and smoked sausages and fish and salads and imagining their flavours: and spending far too much money. She moved to the bakery section, stood sniffing greedily at the aroma of warm bread, then took a bag of croissants, a couple of squishy-looking cream buns, a torte and a large slab of rich chocolate cake. She wandered the aisles, filling her trolley with whatever took her fancy.

She wheeled her way to the checkout. The whole haul came to an astronomical amount. But who cared? She wrote a cheque with a flourish, then began to pack everything into carrier bags. Her mother would care, she realised suddenly. ('Always make a list beforehand and never shop when you're hungry. Otherwise you only waste money on impulsive buys.') 'Fuck my mother,' Sue thought, then started guiltily at the idea. She tossed her head to dispel the notion, but all the same her pleasure in her purchases was just that little bit dimmed.

Back at the flat she spent an agreeable fifteen minutes opening packets and considering what to eat in which order. She decided on the croissants with apricot jam and brie, plus strong, freshly-ground coffee followed by some Greek yoghurt.

After she'd demolished that lot she began on one of the cream buns; and was half-way through it when she discovered she had eaten quite enough. She tossed the remainder of the bun in the bin.

Now she should put the shopping away: at least stow the perishables in the fridge. ('Always clear up as you go, it's quicker in the long run.') But, what the hell, she was sick of food. She wandered out into the garden.

Oh! Look! Terrific! The lilac was beginning to bud; she imagined the heady scent of its blossom. She wandered further. The lawn was looking a little patchy; should she aerate it, fertilise and reseed?

No. She'd a far better idea. She'd dig up that bald bit, turn it into a square bed and fill it with the annuals she had grown from seed. The seedlings had wilted, leggily, for quite long enough in their peat pots on the coffee table under the living room window; they were becoming an eyesore.

Sue dug. She rested and surveyed her handiwork. She glanced at her watch, Good Lord, the time! She returned indoors, stepped over the bags of shopping on the floor and rinsed the soil from her fingers at the sink. The seedlings were still in their peat pots but she didn't have a moment. Because, if she were quick, she could just manage a trip to Compendium to see what was new on the fiction shelves and still be back for the omnibus edition of *Brookside*. What would Mick and Josie be up to this week? she wondered. She paused, her hands still outstretched under the mixer tap. After she watched *Brookside* she might stick with the television for *Blind Date* and then *Inspector Morse*. Or she might read one of the books she was bound to have bought. She'd probably buy the new P.D. James, she decided. Or a Sara Paretsky. She might cook herself a delicious meal and read as she ate. A good job she'd picked up that bottle of Chardonnay; it would go down a treat with, for instance, a grilled trout. But she hadn't bought a trout; no matter, she'd pass the fishmongers on the way.

Compendium. She selected her books, then passed a display stand on which stood several copies of a fat, rather badly-designed paperback. Across the front of it was printed in large letters, 'Alice Mayer's Dictionary.' Could it be the same Alice? Surely not.

Sue picked up a copy and flicked through it. And yes, 'burglar' was defined to take account of the conversation she had with Alice — how long ago now? — after that prat Peter left. So perhaps it could be? She added the book to her haul.

At home she switched on the TV; she crossed to the sofa

intending to make herself comfortable. She tripped on the pile of books she'd tumbled from her hand luggage the previous Sunday night; she subsided with a thump. And there, next to her on the sofa, were her notes on how to murder her mother. She picked them up, read them and a fresh wave of anger boiled over her.

For now that she came to consider the evidence in the cold light of day, it pointed more and more to the conclusion that her mother had been right. And not just because of that incident in Russia.

She had been right about Lawrence and she had been right about Alice: certainly both of them had pissed off somewhere. Sue didn't mind about Lawrence taking off — about Lawrence as Lawrence that is; she should have kicked him out ages ago. But she sure as hell would mind if he'd left for the reason her mother put forward. ('It's always a mistake to make the first move. You could get yourself into all sorts of trouble. Besides, men like to feel a woman's a challenge. They won't respect you.')

Lawrence had been a mistake all right. Lawrence was a wimp. But the fact remained that she was the one who suggested they move in together and he was the one who left. ('I won't say I told you so, but you have become very headstrong and no man wants a woman ruling the roost. They have their pride. And after all, what could you expect? For ever leaving him on his own.')

As for Alice, oh well! Sue sighed. No doubt Alice had her reasons.

Sue picked up a pen. 'Motive,' she added to her list. She underscored it hard. She turned to a fresh page. ('No need to waste all that paper, surely dear?')

'Jealousy?' Definitely not. Who would want to be her mother, alone — since Sue's father's death — in that huge house with all those couches and chintz curtains and cake forks and doilies and fish knives, like something out of Betjeman? Who would want to live in a world where meals were always on time and very little happened in between?

'Revenge?' For having taught Sue all those rigid rules which now returned to haunt her?

No. The reason was: she needed to stop her mother being right again. For now that it turned out she was right about smoking in the street, what was to stop her from being right about all those other things?

The television was still on; Josie was shouting at Mick, but Sue hadn't a clue what about. She'd probably missed the best part. She flung down her list, rose, crossed the room and snapped off the set. Should she go to the kitchen and cook the trout? Should she open the bottle of Chardonnay which she had failed to chill?

She shook her head. She would go straight to Muswell Hill. By Tube to Highgate and walk from there . . . Immediately. And she would take the bread knife. She picked up the Adam Dalgliesh and stuffed that in her bag too to read on the way; the Misery Line always took so long. She left, slamming the door.

In the huge house in Muswell Hill the light was fading in the big, old-fashioned, ultra-clean kitchen. Sue's mother had, as usual, eaten early, had drunk (in the lounge) a cup of tea, had washed the cup and saucer and all the other things, dried them, put them away, closing each cupboard with a satisfying click. She wiped the worktops, wrung out the cloth, stepped outside, pegged it on the line and returned indoors.

'What did you have for tea, Mum?' asked Sue. She was leaning her elbow on one of the counters. ('Don't do that dear, you're bound to leave a mark.')

'Just out of interest? Was it long ago you ate? The kitchen's always so tidy you wouldn't think you ever ate. But you did, didn't you? I'll bet you had cucumber sandwiches and Madeira cake, right?' ('Always a light meal in the evening and always before eight if you want to avoid upsets in the night.')

But Sue asked all these questions because she knew that after death, the time of death was frequently determined by the nature and the stage of digestion of the contents of the stomach of the deceased.

Sue wandered around the kitchen, taking care not to touch the spotless surfaces with her hands. No dust on which to leave visible fingerprints but that didn't matter nowadays; they sprinkled the entire scene of the crime with a white powder which threw previously undetectable marks into sharp relief.

'I was just wondering, Mum,' she said. 'Last time I was here I think I left a pair of gloves. Rather good black leather gloves. They're not in here. Of course, you'll have tidied them. I'll pop up to my old room and check, if that's okay?' ('Always leaving things lying around. Treat the house like a hotel when you do turn up. Expect your old room to be there waiting for you.')

Sue found the gloves. She slipped them over her hands, smoothing out the wrinkles from each fine-skinned finger. She admired the heavy silver buckles at the wrists.

Downstairs, in the lounge, Sue's mother was sitting propped upright in a chintz chair, knitting. 'I was so pleased to find them,' Sue held up her gloved hands, 'that I put them on.' ('Very nice. Not for wearing indoors, though. Aren't those silver attachments a little, well . . . masculine. Still, I suppose they go with your slacks.')

Was her mother's knitting, Sue wondered, long enough, strong enough to strangle her? Probably not.

Sue hovered in the doorway ('Do sit down dear, enough to make anyone nervous'). Sue dithered. ('Make up your mind, now. You must be either coming or going.')

So Sue made up her mind, it was as simple as that. It was as simple as going into the kitchen, fetching the bag which held the bread knife, returning to the lounge, and — from behind — plunging the knife deep into her mother's flesh.

Sue's mother's body jerked. Her hands flew up. Her needles leapt into the air, stitches dropped. She emitted a sharp 'O!' as Sue's knife struck bone.

Blood gushed. Sue looked down, saw the pale silk of her mother's dress embedded in the edges of the wound and, with a shriek of her own, tried to withdraw the knife. But its serrations held it firm in the flesh. She struggled with it as she would the cork of a wine bottle, bracing herself, then decided better to plunge it in, twist it, put her mother out of her misery.

At last the two of them collapsed, linked by the knife, onto the Kossett carpet. Sue's mother twitched, then lay still. Sue stepped back. She looked at the corpse, the skirt of its silk dress tangled around its thighs, exposing the thick, brown tops of SuppHose and one white tab of the suspender of its Latex 'belt'. Sue bent over and tugged down the skirt to a decent length.

She straightened. In the decapitation scenario she would now remove her mother's head, saw it off, using the same serrated knife. Afterwards, her mother's head would sit on the floor beside the nest of tables — fortunately unbroken by the death throes — leaking from the neck, eyes glazing, hair matted with blood. But the serrated bread knife, she recalled, was stuck immovable in her mother's back. She abandoned the idea.

Sue paced along the dark pavement of broad, curved Muswell Hill Road. To her left, behind a high wooden fence, the trees of

Highgate nodded dark limbs against the fire-red glow which always hangs over even the darkest of London's streets. To her right lay Queen's Wood, in which, further down the hill, the victims of the Great Plague lay buried in their hundreds, possibly thousands, in mass, unidentified graves. Unlike Susan's mother, their bodies were long since fleshless. Would they, now, be even so much as skeletons? Or would they be a mass of femur, tibia, sternum and clavicle, as tangled in death as their limbs were when they were tipped, at the end of their last, torchlight journey, from the putrid carts?

In those days, Sue reflected, the disposal of a body in the house would be a simple matter. Paint a red cross upon the door. Write 'Lord have mercy on us' below it and sit back and wait to hear the bells ringing, for the carts to come. How many murders, she wondered, had been committed, back in the seventeenth century, and concealed as death by plague?

Her mood lightened as she considered this. Nearly 70,000 people had died in the Plague, she'd read. What percentage in suspicious circumstances?

She wondered why no one had ever written a mystery about it; it was the sort of plot she'd expect Josephine Tey to have picked up on years ago. And while she was wondering, she arrived at the Broadway. Now what? Where would she go?

She would go to the pub which her mother had always hated. The one with all the clutter.

The pub was empty. Sue bought a whisky, then settled at a table against the wall. She took out her Adam Dalgliesh, placed in on the table, but did not open it. Instead she looked at the clutter. Horse brasses on the crossbeams, toby jugs and miniatures on the shelves, badges and postcards and pennants pinned to the walls. Looking at clutter was curiously soothing in much the same way that travelling was. She raised her eyes. The lion's share of the clutter was suspended from the ceiling. She studied the objects, then closed her eyes and tried to remember them one by one.

'Pelmanism,' said a man's voice.

Sue kept her eyes closed. Most of them went away if you ignored them.

'How many did you remember?' the voice continued.

And some of them didn't. She opened her eyes.

'Know what that is?' he asked. She swivelled her head to follow his pointing finger.

'No.' She swivelled it back to look at him. He was tall. He had thick, black hair. He had a broad, crooked nose, which looked as though it had once been broken. He wore a black leather jacket.

'A flange.'

Under the jacket he wore a black tee-shirt: a thin black tee-shirt through which she could see the contours of his abdomen.

'And that one,' he gestured to a three-legged iron pot, 'is a raddle pot. Raddle, in case you don't know, is the red dye for marking sheep to show who they belong to. And that one . . .' he pointed to a much bigger iron pot with a handle but no legs, 'is a spider. Common in the US. To be filled with hot fat and used for frying doughnuts. And that one . . .'

He had an attractive voice: an engaging smile.

'All right,' said Sue, 'You don't have to go on.'

'. . . is a griddle. Also from New England. A frying pan to us.' He paused. 'I'm just going to get a drink,' and left for the bar. Sue put her fingertips together and rested her chin on them. She watched the man as he stood at the bar; he wore blue jeans; had small buttocks and narrow hips; he was probably a good dancer.

The man returned. He pulled up a chair and settled himself on it. He looked down at his glass. 'As I say,' he continued, 'a griddle.'

'And that . . .' he turned his attention again to the ceiling, 'is a World War Two gas mask.' He lifted a finger to point. 'And that is an original Coca-Cola bottle. And that is a stirrup iron with a safety catch. And that is . . .' He stopped, took a sip of beer, replaced his glass on the table, reached across and touched her on the knuckle, very briefly, with his index finger, then retracted his hand and ran it round the rim of his glass. 'I don't know about your name,' he said, 'but I'm afraid mine's Rudolph.'

'Oh dear.' Sue drooped the corners of her mouth obligingly. 'How did you end up with that?'

'My mother was a silent movie buff. Hooked on Valentino.'

'So you had a mother, too.'

They talked on. Not about the subjects people should discuss when they first meet ('And what do you do? I'm in the retail trade. Oh, really? I'm in advertising.') No: Sue and Rudolph talked about things that would enable them to make slightly personal — and in a veiled way, complimentary — remarks about each other; they talked about Rudolph Valentino and about Susan Sontag (Sue had given Rudolph her name by then and was on to her second whisky) and about little-friend-Susan in the Milly-Molly-Mandy books.

'But nowadays,' Rudolph gestured at Sue's P.D. James. 'Nowadays you read crime?'

She nodded. 'I like exciting plots. Proper adventures.'

'Me too, Though I read science fiction mostly.'

After a third whisky and a good deal more talk, Sue gathered her belongings and rose to leave. Rudolph rose too. They left together.

They walked along the road. Rudolph offered Sue a Silk Cut. She took one, then realised she was smoking in the street. She smoked on.

They walked past Highgate Tube Station. Sue went on walking. She went on smoking.

'I don't know how you feel about the idea,' said Rudolph. 'But I was going to pick up a takeaway and then maybe watch a video. My flat,' he explained, 'is only just round the corner.' He smiled. 'If you're anything like me you've never anything in on Saturday.'

Sue had a fleeting vision of the groceries on the floor in the kitchen, of the trout leaking onto the Sara Paretsky in the carrier bag in the living room, then turned her attention to visualising the contents of her bag.

A couple of Lil-lets. A phonecard. Her cheque book. Her Barclay and Access cards. Her driving licence. Her pocket diary. A purse with at least half a dozen five-pound notes crammed inside.

She thought again, hard. Yes, she was sure she had some condoms in there too.

She nodded. 'Why not?'

They rented the video; *Terminator*, they decided, was a good compromise between their tastes. They chose the pizza. They bought a bottle of Minervois. They headed for Rudolph's place.

The frontage of his block wasn't particularly prepossessing: early sixties, Labour council, by the look of it. Nor was the hallway: piles of junk mail, lino on the floors, a faint smell of decay which reminded her of Russia. He led her upstairs. He unlocked a door. He conducted her along a narrow, dim corridor. 'This is it,' he said, and ushered her, flicking on the light, into an extraordinary, crowded room.

So much so it took Sue a moment or two to distinguish one object from another. Dozens of dark-framed paintings loomed from the walls; a lion's head glared from the top of a large, mahogany chest of drawers; a quantity of oriental-looking figurines in tarnished bronze thronged the shelves in the alcoves; several oddly-shaped sculptures in coloured glass squatted on a huge, dark desk; a brace of pistols hung over the unlit gas fire; a pair of high, brown riding boots buckled with sharp, silver spurs stood in front of it; and in the centre of the room, on the thick, patterned carpet, stood a gaunt, functional-looking chair with a black leather seat and several apparently functionless attachments of shiny, tubular steel.

'I collect things,' explained Rudolph. 'Take a seat.' He waved at a sofa which was covered with some sort of animal skin. Sue sat. What could the chair be for? she wondered. Rudolph opened the wine and filled two glasses; one of the glasses was a fluted goblet, the other was a solid-looking blue tumbler. He handed Sue the goblet. The two of them ate and drank. But while they did so, Rudolph, instead of slotting the video into the VCR which stood, with a small TV, on an ornate metal tea trolley, began to speak about the various objects around them.

'The lion's head I bought in a roadside shop in Hampshire,' he informed her. 'I was quite taken aback when I came across it. The pistols — would you believe it? — I picked up in a car boot sale; that was some time ago now. The riding boots are genuine army issue. See those spurs?'

Sue nodded.

'The glass is mainly deco,' he went on. 'You might want to take a closer look at it later. One or two of the pieces . . .' he spoke into his blue tumbler, 'are rather unusual. Would fetch a fair price, if I ever wanted to sell them, as erotic art. If you look at them from the right angle, that is. Same goes for some of the figurines.' He waved his hand at the shelves.

Sue carried on eating.

'And the chair,' he persisted, 'I bet you don't know what the chair is?'

Sue shook her head.

'Dentist's chair. I liked the shape. It tilts back. Odd, don't you think?'

Sue nodded again.

'And this . . .' he picked a small cylindrical object with a leather loop on the end of it from the elephant's foot stool next to the sofa, 'is lethal. You coil the loop round your wrist . . .' he did so, 'hit the right pressure point and you can paralyse a man just like that.'

'I see,' said Sue.

He unwound the loop and replaced the weapon. 'And this . . . he reached under the sofa and withdrew by its jewelled handle an object which appeared to be a replica of Excalibur complete with ornate scabbard, 'is a genuine Japanese sword.' He rose to his feet, withdrawing the thing from its sheath. The wide curved blade gleamed. 'You'd be amazed how heavy it is,' he went on. 'Here take it. Mind though, because the blade's razor sharp.'

'I don't think so,' said Sue.

Rudolph made a couple of small feints with the sword. 'Watch this,' he said and began to prance, wielding the weapon in a manner which was elegant, stylised and extremely menacing all at once. His eyes grew serious, then expressionless, then fierce as though he were confronting an enemy. At each sweep through the air, the blade made a soft sound. Sue stopped eating and watched in alarm.

A pretty pickle she was in now. She only had herself to blame, of course, just as she had in Russia. Because what it amounted to was she'd picked up an entirely strange man in a pub and gone home with him and now she was cooped up with a maniac — a homicidal one by the look of it. The sword swished from side to side, cutting and thrusting; Rudolph seemed absorbed in his solitary manoeuvres. He spun this way and that; then, having apparently gained an advantage over his foe, he pressed it, pursuing his invisible adversary twice around the dentist's chair, lungeing and ducking, over to the dark desk, then back again until he stood once more, near Sue. He paused, planted his legs apart and raised the blade, grasped in both hands, high over his head as if about to deal the final blow.

Sue did not move. She must keep her cool, just as she had in Russia. No one had helped her on that occasion. She measured the distance to the door with her eyes. Could she make a run for it? And oh dear, why was her mother always right?

The anger which accompanied this thought almost gave her the impetus to rise to her feet. But the sword swished harmlessly down, not even touching the sofa on which she sat, not even pinking the carpet. Rudolph stopped prancing of his own accord, replaced the blade in its scabbard, returned it to its place under the sofa, sat down and grinned at her. 'I do martial arts classes,' he said. 'Twice a week at Highbury Grove. Do you have any hobbies?'

Sue discovered she was holding her breath, let it out in a rush, then stifled a giggle. 'Recently,' she said, 'I go on holidays.' She turned and smiled broadly back at him.

He took a mouthful of pizza and asked, through it, 'Whereabouts?'

'Odd places. I've just been to Russia. I was attacked in the street by a gypsy.'

'What happened?'

'Nothing really. I kept walking and eventually he let go. I'm thinking of China next. Or possibly Tibet. I could see the sky burials.'

'They've always sounded a bit gruesome to me. Can't say I'm too keen on the sight of blood.'

Sue thought of the unused, serrated bread knife in her bag. She thought of her mother a mere few streets away, folding her knitting, making her bedtime tea, filling her hot water bottle, unaware that Sue was even in Muswell Hill. She also thought of Alice's dictionary, thought she would look up 'Mother' and 'Murder' when she arrived home. 'Perhaps you're right,' she agreed.

Rudolph took a sip of wine. 'Do you want to watch the video now?'

'Fine.' Sue nodded. Sue smiled. Because, of course, Sue's mother had not been right at all about smoking in the street. It was only in Russia where cigarettes were rationed and the black market in them flourished and the gypsies would do anything to get hold of even one of them that smoking in the street was wrong — that is to say dangerous. But there would be no harm at all, a little later, in taking a closer look — from the right angle, of course — at those unusual deco pieces and those bronze figurines.

for reference only

There's a myth among the other inmates that we 'fraggles' bay, like dogs, at each full moon. This is not, strictly speaking, true. The noise can — and does — occur on any night: indeed, on every night.

Much of it is mere banging: but there are also the voices, rich in range of pitch and tone. Though not in vocabulary. How long, in here, will my own words last?

Of course, I am not the first to suffer for my muse. Take John Clare. Take Mandelstam. Or take T.S. Eliot. I mention him not because — to my knowledge — he was ever imprisoned, but because a fragment of his work beats over and over in my brain.

In the room the women come and go
Talking of Michelangelo

Why were they talking of Michelangelo? Is it merely that the name rhymed and scanned and that any other renaissance artist who fitted these requirements would have done equally well? Or is there some uniqueness of meaning which lurks below the surface and which I cannot grasp?

'Talking of de de do de do.' My voice rises.

'Hey Shakespeare.' The flap in my door opens and Officer Usbourne peers in. 'Give it a rest, lad. Get some sleep.'

'I don't need sleep.' I look at the section of his face — eyebrows to upper lip — which is visible through the gap. 'I need a dictionary.'

Who took my dictionary? Who took my *Metaphysical Poets*, my copy of *The Waste Land*, my Wordsworth? Was it the first one?

It is only the first one whom I recall with clarity. I was in the lounge, reading Keats and wrestling with an ode of my own when the doorbell chimed. I went into the entrance hall. I opened the door.

A broad, balding man in a shiny suit stood on the steps. 'Mr Moresby?' I nodded. He was, he explained in tones rich with the self-importance of minor officialdom, the bailiff acting on behalf of the VAT Inspectorate. He had powers of entry, he added, then paused. I followed his gaze and looked — as I had not for some time — at the entrance hall.

The carpet was still the wall-to-wall greyish-green, deep pile, which Jeannie had chosen; it was still a shade darker than the marble plant containers which stood either side of the mahogany grandfather clock. But the carpet was stained with the mud I must have tramped in over the months; the dead leaves of swiss cheese plants lay upon it like great, brown, broken plates; newspapers and unopened envelopes silted the bright, white skirting boards.

I showed him into the lounge. 'Splashed out on a leather suite,' he commented. 'A stereo TV. And a CD. Must have cost a pretty penny.'

'I have no money now.' I turned from him, crossed the room and stepped out of the french windows. I slipped between the patio furniture with its thin crusting of velvety green mould. I crossed the wide, wild lawn between the classical, weed-filled urns. I walked the length of the swimming pool on which last year's leaves bobbed like skeletons of tiny boats. I reached the rose garden: I stopped. I pulled the reddest of the buds towards me. I sniffed its fragile petals. I looked deep into its heart, to the centre of its meaning. I wrote my ode.

'Mr Moresby,' says my solicitor, 'you must realise it is no defence to claim you are a poet.'

He tries again. 'Mr Moresby, you had a good life.'

I shake my head. 'The living dead. In comedy, as so often, resides a deeper truth.'

'I beg your pardon?'

'The gibes of Monty Python. The image of accountancy.'

'But your responsibilities. To your clients. Your staff. Your wife!'

'I have no responsibilities. Except to my muse.'

He sighs. 'We'll talk further when we have the psychiatrist's report. Meanwhile, if there's anything you need . . .?'

'I need a dictionary.'

My cell door opens. It is Officer Usbourne. 'Shakespeare.' He takes a couple of steps forward. 'I've been wanting to ask you . . .' He halts, removes his cap and scratches his head. 'Why would anyone become a poet?'

He is a decent man with, so far as I can detect, a genuine interest. So I tell him about the dead cat, lips shrunk back from bared teeth, blank eyes clouding, which I stumbled across in the gutter, one weekend, on my way to my City office.

He shakes his head. 'I don't understand.'

'It was then,' I inform him, 'in those empty, windy streets of my existence that I was confronted with truth: the end of life is death.'

'What of it?'

'Time was short. I left those barren streets for a richer landscape.'

He wrinkles his brow. 'Where did you go?'

'To the world of the imagination.' I pause. 'It was only through poetry, through owning words, that I could own life itself, experience life. What remained of it. To its full extent.'

'But you were pretty well-off by all accounts. Isn't there anything you miss? Anything you need?'

'I need a dictionary.'

'Oh well.' He rises and replaces his cap. 'More chance of that tomorrow once you're out of the psychiatric wing.'

I cannot sleep: because of the prospect of a dictionary. Mind-picture follows mind-picture; but where are the words to make them real? Understanding tugs at the edges of my consciousness like an insistent child at the hem of its mother's skirt. But when I try to grasp it, it — more elf than child — whirls out of reach. Columns of words drift before my eyes. The print shifts and reforms and — like a ripe seed pod — seems about to burst and yield up all its meanings; when the clang of the cell door whisks the patterns away and it is time for slopping out.

I am to share a cell: with a young man with muscled, tattooed arms. Clark.

'What are you in for?' Clark asks.

'They say fraud. That I am a cheat. But I have told them the truth. I have done nothing.'

'Same here.'

Yet Clark is, he admits, an 'old lag'; he knows the ropes.

When I explain about the dictionary: 'Put down for English classes,' he advises.

Within days I am tramping into a classroom: peeling paint on the walls, a dusty blackboard and desks too small for grown men. I squeeze into one. A young woman distributes worksheets. 'Today,' she announces, 'we are doing the comma.'

She is at my elbow. 'How are you with this?'

'I need a dictionary.'

'Not for this.'

'I need to look up . . .' I stab a finger at random at the page.

She sighs. 'Oh, all right,' crosses the room, unlocks a grey metal cupboard and extracts a *Penguin English*. I take it and immerse myself in meaning.

The young woman is at my elbow again. 'Time to finish.' She closes the *Penguin*.

'Could I borrow it?'

'No. For reference only,' and locks it away.

'It is not enough,' I complain to Clark later, 'to have occasional access to words. I need to keep them.'

On Wednesday I meet the librarian, Lawrence. He tries to be helpful, but resources are limited; and dictionaries are, once again, for reference only. Instead he offers me a book on mid-life crisis. It's not unusual, he assures me, for someone of my age to throw up everything, to seek to 'find' himself. Men have biological clocks too.

'But suppose,' I ask him, 'I *was* meant to be Prince Hamlet?'

'Oh yes. Prufrock. I'm sure I have some Eliot somewhere.'

But I no longer want to read other poets. I want a dictionary because a dictionary contains *all* the words. It contains all the meanings. Must it not, therefore, contain the answers? If only I could wrest them out?

Best he can offer, he says, is that he occasionally supplements his stock by buying, out of his own pocket, second-hand books from a junk shop. He'll keep an eye open.

But it is Clark who hands me a volume. 'It's doing the rounds,' he says.

Why? Are dictionaries that much in demand?

'Written by a woman.' He leers. 'Hot stuff. Look up "volcano". Or "whoosh". The big "O". He winks. I ignore his obscure innuendo and barter my watch for the book.

I sit on my bunk and turn the pages. The dictionary is compiled by Alice Mayer. I remember an Alice Mayer from school. But never mind that; the words are what I need.

I recall the rosebud in my garden and the meaning I detected at its heart. I recall the forest of Epping outside the gates of my house. And — now that I have the words — I apprehend that beneath my feet the bracken is of burnished gold, fragile, friable. Beyond, a wide expanse of grass shivers green — and silver from the dew — under the numinous, pellucid glow of an enervated, equinoctal sun. The etiolated undersides of aspen leaves whisper and tinkle like a crystal chandelier. Yes: in owning the words I own the world.

And I am utterly alone.

That was my 'crime'. To be alone and to be a poet: to be alone on the black, rich earth of the forest paths, to inhale the damp, peaty, fungoid odour of the leaf mould, the toasty essence of the dying ferns, the thin, resinous scent of pines. Whilst, in my hallway, the brown and white rectangles of bills and summonses and court orders silted, among the great, brown, broken leaves of the swiss cheese plants, against the white skirting board.

But they will not let me be alone. They demand that I rise and shave and eat. And Clark demands the return of the dictionary.

'One week only,' he says. 'There's a waiting list.'

So even contraband words are not mine to keep.

They say I need further medication. I say nothing. They say I need closer observation. They return me, wordless, to the psychiatric wing.

The long nights crawl by. They are filled with voices, but the words are not my own.

The brief days pass. During one of them the flap of my cell door opens and, 'Haven't forgotten you,' Lawrence announces cheerfully, passing, through the gap, a battered book. 'Couldn't lay my hands on a dictionary, but an encyclopedia's almost as good, surely? Even if it is a children's one?'

I open the volume. It contains the answers to a series of 'Did You Know' Encyclopedic quiz books. There are no questions. I raise my eyes — meet Lawrence's eager ones, see the bridge of his nose, his black moustache. When I tell him what he has brought the moustache droops with the downturn of his upper lip. 'I only glanced at the cover,' he apologises. 'Had no idea.'

But the book has the answers. 'And I *can* keep them?' He nods.

When I am alone: 'The egg is laid on an under-water stem of the plant,' I read. 'Manila, hemp, cotton, jute, sisal.' 'Lancelot, Gawain, Gareth, Galahad,' 'Renaissance', 'The natterjack' and — my favourite — 'The rod of lead is placed in one grooved half; then the other half is glued on.'

happy endings

Alice was going to give a party.

Words for a party: a function, a launch, a reception, a crush, a bit of a do, a knees-up, a bash.

Alice's party was not going to be a bash or a crush or a knees-up, anyone could hold one of those; it was going to be an adult, piss-elegant affair.

In a sense, though, the party *was* a function, that is, it *had* a function. It was going to be a belated launch for her dictionary. But Alice was also giving the party for personal reasons.

The first thing Alice was going to do about the party was to look forward to it. That was part of the fun. After that she would start planning.

The plans.

Clothes. She had nothing special except the Dave Godwin-tarnished red mini and she wasn't going to wear that. Besides, it wasn't piss-elegant.

She was going to wear a pair of baggy knee-length shorts of green jersey, patterned in dark red, tailored at the waist, with five little buttons up the front like a pair of Levi 501s, except those buttons were black. And thick green tights and either black lace-up ankle boots or, if she could find them, green ones like a pixie's. And possibly a rather expensive plain green shirt in brushed cotton with fullish sleeves and no cuffs.

Alice didn't own any of these clothes, although she had seen the shorts on a rack beside a stall in Camden Lock. Buying the clothes was going to be part of the fun.

Venue. As it was going to be an elegant party, no one would spill drinks or stub cigarettes out on the carpet; which meant, and if she didn't invite too many people, she could hold it in her flat.

Guests. She would send personal invitations to: all the people at Holdman and Ray's — that equalled five. Melissa, Clara and Trudi, eight. Miss Burrows and Gerald, ten. Dave Godwin, she really should as he was responsible for the grant which made the dictionary possible; she could keep him at arm's length. Oh and Victoria Day and Milly Moxon, why not?

Thirteen. Unlucky. She'd invite Bruno Barkworth. Fourteen was a perfectly good basis for a party.

She was worried though as to whether the balance would be right. Too many women? Too many men? And why didn't she have any friends from the ethnic minority communities?

No matter. The invited guests were only the start. She was going to put an ad in *City Limits* in the poetry section; that's how proper publishers did it. She also discovered, from going to launches in local bookshops that, unless you were Fay Weldon, say, you couldn't expect more than a handful of people to turn up on spec. Say ten. To be on the safe side, say thirty all told.

How many bottles of wine? Six glasses to a bottle. This wasn't going to be a drunken occasion, so say three glasses each, max. Glasses would be on sale or return from the offie. And perhaps she could wear black culottes with a plain white blouse? And several chunky silver rings? That would be piss-elegant.

Alice worded her advertisement carefully; the party was to run from 7.00 for 7.30 to 9.30 p.m. to make it quite clear this was an early evening, not an open ended affair. She headed it 'Dictionary Launch' to deter casual partygoers. 'Drinks will be served,' she added. Then she posted it.

Her colleagues in Dictionaries and Diaries all said they'd come. Alice wondered about music. It was a good idea to provide some sort of background, at least to start with. Light classical, she supposed, neither too bouncy nor too heavy. Mozart? Haydn? And should she, after all, wear a short skirt and sheer tights and be elegant in a Selina Scott-ish way?

Miss Burrows and Gerald accepted by return of post. Milly Moxon left a blurred message on Alice's answerphone saying just try stop her; Victoria Day, Bruno Barkworth, Melissa, Trudi and Clara all rang to say they'd love to. And whatever she wore it must be something with a neat waist. Nothing long that would flap in a tangle around her ankles. She wanted to feel free and comfortable as well as show herself off, look smart.

But first she must tackle the most unpleasant of the preparations. A party, she considered as she scrubbed at the limescale in the loo, up and down, with a long-handled, plastic brush, for the person who holds it is: a reason to scour the dirtiest corners, to clear up the squalidest mess, to chuck out the piles of junk you no longer need.

A party is also an occasion to look forward to, a goal to aim for. A party is a means of taking stock, of redefining one's environment, one's appearance, one's ideas. A party is a form of punctuation, the end of one paragraph in one's life, the beginning of another. A party is a statement about oneself. A party is an act of bravery.

Alice stopped defining in her head, finished cleaning the loo and set about redefining the flat.

.

A party, to Fiona, was a leap in the dark. Who knew whom she might meet this evening at Alice's? she wondered, as she puffed powder onto her cheeks and leaned forwards to check her face more closely in the mirror. She leaned back and looked around her room: the room to which she might bring back the man she might meet.

Soft light from the table lamp, diffused by the pink shade, fell on the pink satin of the cover of the single bed, on the scatter cushions in toning shades, some heart-shaped, some square, some patchwork, some embroidered, some tapestry: all the fine work of Fiona's own hands. And it fell on dear old Snotty Bear.

But Snotty Bear made her think of the past and she mustn't do that. She rose, picked him up, kissed him on his boot-button nose and tucked him away in the wardrobe. 'It's only for tonight,' she assured him as she made him comfortable on a pile of pink pillow cases. 'Besides, I'll probably end up with only you to cuddle after all.' She closed the wardrobe door and returned to the mirror.

Yes, she looked fine, dressed for the man she might meet in a crisp black lace cocktail frock with a low neck and a scalloped hem. She clasped her pearls around her throat, removed the everyday studs from her ears and inserted her pearl and diamante drops.

She glanced at her watch. Nearly time to meet Rosemary.

A few days ago, in the office loo, 'I couldn't go to a party on my own,' Fiona confessed.

Rosemary was scornful. 'You'll know loads of people. Everyone from work will be there.'

'Yes. Still.'

And Rosemary — thank goodness — though she tossed her head, said okay, six-thirty at Earls Court.

Fiona slipped into her coat, crossed to the door, switched off the light, switched it on again, crossed to the wardrobe, opened the door, kissed Snotty on his boot-button nose, closed the wardrobe and left.

In Alice's flat the living room was empty. The furniture was against the walls, copies of the dictionary were stacked on the tops of the bookshelves, Mozart was on the stereo, rows of glasses gleamed and bottles of wine stood open on the dining table ready for the guests.

But Alice was in the bedroom, in front of the full-length mirror.

She was pleased with the black culottes, she decided; they were absolutely right with the black lurex top she had worn to the office do. She was pleased with the black ankle boots; and the sheer black tights; and the two heavy silver rings on the fingers of her right hand; and the new, off-the-face arrangement of her hair. She looked sharp, she looked smart. Alice nodded. She looked her own woman.

All that now remained was to check each room, make sure there was a clean towel in the bathroom, that the top was on the toothpaste, do a final trawl for any evidence of messy personal habits.

Earl's Court station. Fiona glanced about her. But it was all right, there was Rosemary, only a couple of minutes late. She was wearing her leather mini skirt, Fiona noticed; and all her bangles.

As they bought their tickets: 'How come you can't handle

going out alone?' asked Rosemary. 'Thought you lived on your tod?'

Fiona nodded. 'It's only social occasions. I was, well, used to going places with my husband. He was very protective.'

'Tough.' Was there a note of sympathy in Rosemary's usually brusque voice? 'Gets me down too, sometimes, having to look out for myself the whole time.'

Alice discovered she was in the living room, rearranging her hair in front of the mirror over the mantel. She discovered she was in the bedroom, peering under the bed for overlooked scraps of rubbish. She discovered she was in the kitchen, scrubbing madly with a Brillo pad at a hardly visible spot of grease. She discovered she was speeding with the excitement of the anticipation and that she had better slow down.

A change of music was what Alice needed, Alice decided. Mozart was far too upbeat. She went into the living room and inspected her tapes. Leonard Cohen would be just right; she slotted him into the stereo.

At King's Cross Rosemary and Fiona changed to the Northern Line. To the Northern Line platform, that was, no sign of a train and the indicators were out again. They waited. Over the tannoy a voice began a garbled justification of the delay.

As they waited, they swapped life stories.

'Gosh,' said Fiona to Rosemary, 'I never realised you were married too. How long ago was your divorce?'

'Oh ages.' Rosemary shrugged, then pointed at the indicator

board. 'Look, one for Highgate in thirteen minutes. When was yours?'

'Actually, I'm still married.'

Alice rather wished she wasn't about to give a party, that she was about to sit on the sofa for the evening, one knee crossed neatly over the other, and enjoy the unaccustomed sparkling splendour of the flat with only Leonard Cohen for company. She reminded herself of her reasons for holding the affair, counting them off on her fingers. Yes, that's why she was giving a party. But why did people come to parties, supposing they did come? When she was a kid she went because she was told to, or for the jelly and ice cream or to become as overexcited as she just had. As a teenager she went to pull boys. But after that? And now?

What, in other words, was the definition of a party as far as a guest was concerned? A mating ritual? An excuse to get out of the house? A chance to get drunk?

I, Richard Moresby, poet and fraggle, am free. I am free and am with Jeannie. I am free and I am with Jeannie in my old home which Jeannie has reclaimed to almost its pristine state. I have Jeannie — or to be precise, Jeannie's father — to thank for my freedom, however brief it may transpire to be.

I have not thanked her. But I have invited her to accompany me this evening to meet the woman who wrote the dictionary to which I owe my continuing and increasing prowess as a poet.

.

Alice looked at her watch. Only fifteen minutes to go and she hadn't finished her last check yet. But no one ever arrived on time; the earliest she could expect people would be a quarter past.

The doorbell rang. She hoped it wasn't a Jehovah's Witness.

On Alice's step stood two women.

A black-gloved hand still pressing the bell. A sharp-featured face. Short, spiky blonde hair. Black leather gear. 'Sue!' Alice cried and flung her arms around her old schoolfriend.

Sue returned the hug. 'Saw the ad in *City Limits*,' she explained. 'I had no idea you were still at the same flat. Otherwise I'd have been in touch. Why didn't you ever answer my messages?'

'Oh, that's ages ago,' Alice waved away the past with one hand. 'Come on in.'

Sue did. 'You've met my Mum, haven't you?'

'Of course.' Alice recognised the rigidly waved grey hair and the thin, disapproving mouth from way back. 'Can I take your coats?'

She put them on the bed. Back in the living room she looked at Sue and her mother looking at the piles of dictionaries. Sue was wearing skin tight leather trousers and a fine black leather top with a high neck and cap sleeves and which ended in a V just below her breasts. Her midriff was bare but her hands were covered in black leather gloves which were, in turn, covered with knobbly silver rings.

Sue's mother was wearing a floral dress with a permanently pleated skirt and self belt. She was wearing a discreet pearl brooch above her right breast. She was wearing navy blue high-heeled court shoes.

Leonard Cohen was droning on about someone giving

someone else head on an unmade bed. Alice crossed the room, switched him off and said into the silence, 'What can I get you to drink?'

'A sherry,' said Sue's mother, 'Amontillado if you have it.'

'I meant red or white.'

Sue dumped herself on one of the upright chairs against the wall. 'White'll be closest. Red for me.' Then she said, just like old times, 'Spit it out. What have you been up to? Besides the dictionary?'

Sue's mother accepted her glassful, then placed it, untouched, on the table. 'What a pleasant flat. And very nicely kept, dear.'

Alice said, 'Do sit down.' And, 'Sue, I don't know where to begin.'

'At the beginning. Don't mind Mum. She'll know the right thing to do while we're having a gossip.'

'If I could just freshen up before the guests arrive . . .?'

Was the top on the toothpaste? Alice wondered as she watched Sue's mother leave the room. And why had they arrived so early?

'Thought you might need some moral support,' explained Sue. 'Now, come on, out with it.'

But instead of filling in the gaps since they met, they found themselves reminiscing about people they both once knew at school. Which was a delight, but an indulgence and not the right preparation, Alice felt, for an evening intended to make a statement about who she was in the here and now.

The doorbell rang. She went to open it. 'Oh hello, Lawrence. Sue's already arrived.' Alice ushered him into the living room.

Sue looked up sharply. 'What do you think you're doing here?'

'Much right as anyone else. That was an open invitation in

City Limits. Besides, I was the one who gave her the advice about the insurance.'

Alice looked from one to the other. 'So you two aren't . . .' she began, then added quickly. 'No, of course, I can see you aren't any more. Sue, do choose some music. Lawrence, what would you like to drink?'

The doorbell rang again. Alice hoped for the crowd from Holdman and Ray's. She hoped for any crowd: to dilute the hostility.

But it was Dave Godwin. He joined the others, said hello, took a glass of wine from Alice, put his arm round her shoulder and kissed her cheek. 'Knew you'd want me here early,' he confided, 'so we could welcome the guests together.'

'Ha!' said Sue, 'so that's what's been happening since we last met.'

'No it hasn't,' said Alice.

Then: 'Expecting quite a crowd, are you, dear?' asked Sue's mother.

Alice wished she hadn't set out all two dozen glasses.

The doorbell rang. Alice set off across the uncrowded room, then down the long empty hallway.

It was Joey, a bunch of flowers in one hand, a box of Milk Tray in the other. 'And all because the lady loves . . .' he said, then went on: 'But seriously, I did try to get hold of you at work. I did phone several times. Then when I saw the ad . . .' He paused in the living room doorway, thrust the flowers at her and kissed her cheek. He looked up at the others. 'A select gathering,' he commented, keeping his arm around her shoulder. 'Well, do introduce me.'

But before she could do so she was surrounded. By Henry, by Douglas, by Fiona and Rosemary, by Timothy, Miss Burrows,

Gerald, Melissa, Clara, Trudi, several men from the bookbinding plant, Bruno Barkworth and a quantity of middle-aged men in flowered shorts whom Bruno introduced as his friends. 'Oh gosh,' muttered Alice as she shook hands, one after the other, with the entire Patel family from round the corner, 'did I leave the door open?'

'No idea about security,' butted in Lawrence. 'And look who you've let in.' He nodded in the direction of a heavily-built man in a sleeveless denim jacket and a sweat band round his long, dark hair. 'Peter!' said Alice.

Bert Langley and Greg Wale were sitting side by side in the back seat of a minicab. The minicab was stuck in a traffic jam in Graham Road, E8. 'Should have sussed this, you should,' Bert, leaning forward, admonished the driver.

'Bloody roadworks,' replied the man.

'Funny you should say that.' Bert settled back in his seat. 'Have you heard the one about Robert Maxwell and the traffic cones on the M25?' But Greg shook his head and advised him to save his gags for the party.

Bert nodded. 'Should be plenty of the right people there. Told you that when I saw it in *City Limits*.' For Bert had spotted, several days before, Alice's ad. 'Hey lookee here,' he announced, rocking the rickety formica-topped table in his excitement.

'Funny you mentioned Alice Mayer the other evening. She's published a book.'

So Alice must be famous after all, they decided. Which was why, tonight, the two of them, in their sharpest of suits, set off for her party.

Milly Moxon was sitting in the same traffic jam as Bert and

Greg, but she wasn't in a minicab, oh no. Milly always took a black taxi, she could be sure they'd done the Knowledge, knew where they were going.

She leant forward intending to ask the driver why the fuck they had stopped for so long, nearly lost her balance, recovered, leant back and knocked, delicately, on the glass in front of her. Had to be careful of her movements after she'd had a few; but only a very few tonight, and only white wine.

'Yes, lady?'

'What the fuck's going on?'

He turned to look at her. Milly, she knew, was a picture for her age. She knew that anyway by the way the cabbie's eyes lingered.

Which was why, no doubt, he made no comment on her language. And which was why, no doubt, they started chattering away like old friends. Or possibly like old lovers.

Alice was pouring wine and dropping in on conversations. 'Good Lord,' Sue exclaimed, 'it's Reedy Richard from primary school. Mum, you remember Richard?'

'Yes, dear. Such a smart little boy. And what have you been up to all these years?'

'I've just come out of prison.'

'Well,' said Sue quickly. 'Better in than out, I dare say.'

'I'm only on bail. I'll be back inside as soon as I've been to court. After they prove me guilty.'

'What I ask,' said Rosemary, 'is did they use unionised labour for this dictionary of hers? And if not, why not?'

'I brought her flowers,' said Joey. 'and a box of Milk Tray. Yet she's hardly given me a glance.'

'The unions,' said Lawrence, 'are the major source of reactionary policies within the Labour Party.'

'Nobody ever brings me flowers,' said Rosemary.

'So you're in my borough,' said Dave Godwin, seizing Henry by the hand. 'Dave Godwin. Deputy Leader of the Council and Chair of the Grants Sub.'

'One of these youngsters with no respect for the past, I dare say. Pull down people's homes and put up tower blocks like a shot.'

'That was in the sixties,' Dave Godwin protested, 'I've only been on the council a couple of years.'

Oh dear, maybe Alice should circulate people, split them up and introduce them to others?

But: 'A fat grey cob called Kate,' Fiona was telling Miss Burrows. 'Rex, my old Shetland. And Brigadoon, the hunter Daddy keeps for me on the offchance.'

'Grey . . .' breathed Elizabeth.

'A refill?' Alice asked.

A gravel drive, Elizabeth imagined, a circular gravel drive, Gerald motoring up to it, to the great house. He stopped the Metro. She climbed out. Fiona was there on the wide steps between the Palladian pillars to welcome her. And Fiona was wearing jodhpurs! 'Let's not bother with Mummy and Daddy right now. We'll have tea with them later. There's Dundee cake.' She linked arms with Elizabeth. 'Let's go straight to the stables.' They did. And there was a square cobbled yard, all spick and span. At the sound of footfalls the horses stuck out their heads from their boxes. Which beautifully groomed neck would Elizabeth pat first? To which horse would she give the first, repeatedly-scrubbed carrot?

'I can't believe you write all your novels in longhand,' Joey said to Victoria Day. 'Don't you realise how much easier it would be with a PC? I'm in the business.'

'Who's not PC?' Rosemary butted in. 'Don't tell me you're another one who reads the *Sunday Times*? Like Alice.' She turned and gave her a dirty look. 'Says she does it for the book reviews.' Alice moved on.

'The rot really set in with Kinnock,' Dave Godwin was telling Lawrence. He stopped, reached out, seized Alice round the waist and held her to his side. 'The Party,' he went on, 'is just another group of grey men.'

'I still feel,' Lawrence demurred as Alice slipped free, 'that hounding the Militants out was a mistake. Not that I have any sympathy with them these days.'

'More of a mistake ignoring the unions,' Rosemary butted in. 'Had to twist Alice's arm over the NUJ, you know that?'

Alice moved on again.

Peter grasped her elbow. 'What's with the formal gear?' he asked. 'You look like you sold out to convention.'

And he looked a mess. Also dated, as though he'd fallen into the party off the stage of a Spinal Tap gig. But why bother telling him? He was old news.

So, 'How's the work going?' she asked.

He shook his head. 'What I need,' he explained, 'is a new medium. Something with the same bulk as word ore. Same capacity for depth and strength. Same variety of texture. Same complexity of strata. But greater plasticity. I feel ready for the experience of moulding.'

'Absolutely,' said Alice.

'Caught up with you at last,' interrupted Sue who was with a thin-hipped man in clothes as black as Alice's. 'You haven't met Rudolph.'

'New Age or no New Age,' Helen, Alice's erstwhile therapist, was saying to Melissa, 'I simply can't approve of these unverified treatments. There's no guarantee you mightn't be doing your clients more harm than good.' Then, spotting Alice, 'Oh there you are. I did feel I ought to put in an appearance. So important with ex-clients who are making a go of things. Any recurrence of those stress-related patterns?'

Alice shook her head.

Timothy informed Sue's mother: 'A proper breakfast, that sets you up for the day.' She nodded. 'Nothing to touch it.' Henry added, 'Meat and two veg of a lunchtime.' Sue's mother agreed, 'Breakfast like a king, lunch like a prince and dine like a pauper.' 'This compulsion to collect artefacts,' Helen told Rudolph, 'you do realise how unhealthy it is?'

Alice grinned. Her party — now — was going a treat. People were doing what they should do — discovering common ground, learning to feel comfortable with each other; and enjoying each other's company. More, they were reaching in their pockets, producing business cards and scraps of paper and scribbling on them and exchanging them. Even Fiona and Miss Burrows were. That was a real sign of a successful affair!

She drifted on.

And here before her was Lewis Black. She didn't recall inviting him, but he was wearing a white dinner jacket and a black bow tie and — my goodness! — didn't he look stunning. No wonder Victoria fell for him.

Bert and Greg were still in their traffic jam. So were the two directors of Holdman and Ray's who had interviewed Alice for her job. So was Milly Moxon. 'Go on,' said Milly, 'it's a man's job to get out and see what the problem is. Why d'you think you've got a dick?' But by this time they were on such good terms he took it as a joke and climbed, goodhumouredly, into the road. He peered ahead, walked a little way and disappeared. Milly lit a Marlboro. The cabbie returned, stuck his head in the window, said, 'No sign of movement anywhere. Maybe a burst water main,' and climbed back in. 'Cigarette?' asked Milly and they resumed their chat.

Bert and Greg's driver was nowhere near as receptive. He failed to laugh at any of Bert's jokes. 'Well we have been here for near on twenty minutes,' said Bert, justifying to Greg why he was wasting his gags.

The directors of Holdman and Ray's were luckier. Their cab driver did a U turn, then an abrupt left, nipped up to Dalston Lane and sped away from whatever it was was causing the holdup, no problem.

Joey said to Victoria, 'I do admire your books. They have the sort of women you want to take care of.'

'Actually,' said Victoria, 'I'm thinking of something quite different next. Science fiction.'

'Ballard,' said a man. 'My name's Rudolph, by the way. And Inglis. Those are my favourites. Plus there's *Dreamside*, which is by a new writer, which you really must read. What's yours about?'

'I thought the planet of Ephemera. A planet that exists only on paper.'

'It would be like the sixties,' Alice said, 'disposable knickers and dresses,' then realised Victoria and Rudolph wanted to talk to each other not her; and moved on.

'Eocene clay.' Peter rubbed his chin and looked down thoughtfully at Henry. 'It might, just might be the medium I'm after.'

Alice looked back at Victoria and Rudolph. Getting on like a house on fire. What about Sue?

'No skin off my nose.' She was at Alice's elbow and looking in the same direction. 'Know what I'm like for moving on.'

'No,' said Alice. Sue explained how after Lawrence pissed off she'd taken up travelling in a big way because she enjoyed the stimulus of new scenery; same went for men.

'And who,' she went on, nodding at Lewis Black, 'is that?'

Alice introduced them.

Alice noticed that Rudolph and Victoria had been joined by Helen, so there could be no harm in her returning.

'It's about lucid dreaming,' Rudolph explained.

'I have this dream of rearranging furniture,' said Alice.

'Oh dear,' said Helen, 'another stress-related pattern.'

'They wouldn't mend the roads,' said Victoria, 'only paper over the cracks.'

Joey turned up once more. 'I don't see the point.'

'The point is that it's a live-for-the-moment sort of world. They don't believe in the value of remembering things, either individually or as a culture. Even their statues are biodegradable. They have a committee which goes round inspecting them and if no one can remember, say, the Duke of Wellington, then they junk the monument.'

'Wouldn't do for me,' Timothy butted in. 'Stickler for tradition and proud of it.'

'Quite correct, dear,' said Sue's mother. 'There's a right way and a wrong way for everything.'

'I rather enjoy remembering things,' said Rudolph. 'I could

close my eyes and recall almost every object on that table.'

'It could be that's a symptom of your compulsion,' said Helen. 'A fear of letting go.'

'I've a jigsaw of Wellington,' said Alice, 'if you'd like to borrow it, Victoria. Oh no, that's Napoleon, wrong horse; you really ought to talk to Douglas. And if you want to know about committees, you should talk to Dave Godwin, he knows exactly how they work. I'll introduce you shall I?' then realised that not everyone came to parties to glean information from other people and shut up.

Alice left them. She surveyed the scene. Apart from being successful (now) this was also, she thought, one hell of a sexy party. There were men everywhere. Lewis: his tie was awry in a curiously attractive fashion — the one imperfection in a perfect man. Rudolph: he had the slimmest of hips, the tightest of buttocks. Dave Godwin was looking sideways at Rosemary in quite the way he used to look at Alice when she thought he looked like Mike; Peter's bare biceps, highly developed from all that heavy work with chunks of word ore, rippled as he raised his glass to his lips; Douglas's sleeves were pushed raffishly up, exposing his forearms; and that man from the bookbinding factory well, a builder's cleavage wasn't so bad after all. He bent to inspect a copy of the dictionary on the coffee table; she saw, in the gap above his trousers, the pale down of gold hair which dusted the tops of his buttocks.

She shook her head, turned back to the table and began to open a bottle of wine.

'Let me do that,' said Joey.

'I am,' said Alice, 'perfectly capable.'

.

The doorbell again. Alice went to answer it. A chinless man with bi-focals and a woman with crimped, yellow hair, peaked nose and creased, cartilaginous neck. What were the two directors of Holdman and Ray's doing here?

Timothy hurried down the hall, hands outstretched, 'All arranged,' he assured them, nodding. He produced his handkerchief, removed his pebble glasses, wiped them, replaced glasses and handkerchief: and whisked the two directors away.

Alice was left to welcome a man with a quantity of cameras slung around his neck.

'Show me the layout, could you?' he demanded. He removed the lens covers from a couple of cameras. 'So I can take a light reading before they start.'

'Who start?' asked Alice, gesturing, for want of anywhere better to gesture, towards the living room. 'Haven't I seen you somewhere before?'

'Dare say. Always where the action is. Don't normally do these in-house magazine assignments. Any idea where she's going to stand?'

'Who?' asked Alice, then remembered. 'You were in Rossi's, with me and Lewis Black and Bruno and Milly and Victoria Day.'

'She here?' The man brightened. He fiddled more vigorously with his lens and his light metre. 'Victoria Day's good copy. Doing anything courageous?'

'I don't know if she'd like . . .' but the man was already in the living room, flashbulbs popping.

Alice followed, slowly. And found her arm grasped by Douglas. 'They want you over here.'

'Where?' asked Alice. 'Who wants?'

He steered her. She found herself facing the bi-focalled

director of Holdman and Ray's. 'Quiet please,' he directed and flopped a copy of Alice's dictionary up and down on the table. It took time for the conversation around them to subside. Then everyone formed a circle, faces politely expectant.

Mr Pettifer shook Alice's hand. He had an unpleasant hand, warm, limp and slightly damp.

He congratulated her on the publication of a most distinctive dictionary. He had an unpleasant voice, rasping.

He presented her with a carriage clock. It was equally unpleasant.

Everyone clapped. The flashbulb popped again. It lit Timothy, beaming. So he was happy, Alice thought.

'Thank you,' she said.

Alice wasn't going to make a speech, no way. She turned to refill a couple of glasses and said in a conversational tone to Henry, 'This'll help me keep track. Won't be late back from lunch again,' and the circle broke up. People straggled up to admire the carriage clock. Timothy told them, 'We had a collection for it. Everyone in the office. To mark the occasion. I organised it of course. You do like it, Alice?'

She nodded.

'Ideal for your mantel,' said Sue's mother.

'Nice bit of gilt,' said Rudolph.

'Nice bit of kitsch,' said Peter.

Said Henry, 'In my day you only received a timepiece when you retired.'

Mrs Landsdowne coughed. 'It is, in fact, something along the lines of a gift of that nature. Don't want to cast a damper. But we would rather you didn't return, Miss Mayer. Not the right calibre for a firm of Holdman and Ray's stature. And that dictionary of yours is a little, shall we say, risqué?' She paused to down a mouthful of Alice's wine. 'A month's money in lieu of notice, naturally. As per the terms of your contract.'

Added Mr Pettifer, looking around the room, 'You're clearly far too busy these days to bother with the daily grind at Holdman and Ray's. Better things to do, humph?'

So Alice was out of a job. And this time no Mike to support her on the proceeds of his stolen goods.

Rosemary butted in — softly because of the proximity of her employers. 'I did warn you. You never completed that application. Only yourself to blame that you haven't the protection of the NUJ.'

Did it matter? Alice wondered. Not really, she decided. She had grown too big for the job now, rather than the job being too big for her. The job was tiny, gosh it was nothing more than a scrap of transparent film on the floor like the remnants of a burst balloon, or like that scrap of cellophane from a cigarette pack just there, on the carpet. She bent, picked it up, crumpled it and tossed it in the waste paper bin.

Mr Pettifer was still by her side. 'Another point,' he said. 'Not that we have a dress code as such. But we do notice these things. Do you always wear trousers?'

'Yes.' Alice paused. 'Why? Don't you?'

'Do you,' she persisted, 'go to work in your knickers? If so, M & S briefs or do you go for boxers? The latter, are considered healthier. Something,' she added, 'to do with the free circulation of air. Good for the cock. Gives it room to breathe.' She wished Milly Moxon were here; Milly would have enjoyed this exchange.

'I think it's time,' said Mrs Landsdowne, 'that we left.'

'I think so too,' said Alice.

In fact it was after nine-thirty. Time for them *all* to leave.

Sue's mother appeared in the living room doorway and began to clear up glasses and plates of peanuts and ashtrays.

Some people took the hint. Along with Pettifer and Landsdowne they gathered up bags and coats and tucked scarves into collars and buttoned coats and buckled belts, smoothing away the wrinkles of fabric under the belts and said goodbye. Alice stood in the doorway, one hand raised, as they left.

She returned to the living room to find the place considerably cleared. Bruno Barkworth and friends were in one corner, turning over her tapes and sorting through her albums.

Alice sat on one of the upright chairs and stretched out her legs. It was over. It had gone well. No one had shouted or got drunk or splashed things on the carpet. Now, pretty soon, the stragglers would leave; then what?

She would rather like a chat with Sue. Only Sue, occupying the sofa, was immersed in conversation with Lewis Black. What were they talking about? Sue's job? Lewis's job? Or one of those irrelevant subjects — soap operas, shopping habits, preference in pets – with which a man and a woman toyed, as with a meal, to fill in the interval between meeting and having sex.

Alice turned her eyes away. Would she ever do that again? Her gaze fell on Dave Godwin who was still arguing with Lawrence and Rosemary. He looked up and she looked away quickly. Yes, of course, she had felt like that with him, but she didn't now. The memory of desire pierced her with the sharpness of pain.

She sighed. Soon a party would be something to look back on instead of something to look forward to.

She didn't want it to be, not yet. She still felt some of that speedy buzz she had before the whole thing began. But surely she had enjoyed herself? It *had* gone off well.

She sighed again. She should bestir herself and give Sue's mother a hand. But no, on second thoughts, why not leave her to it, she was enjoying herself.

The bell rang again. Someone thundered on the door. Alice went to open it. Good God! Who were all these people?

The one in front was Milly Moxon. 'Fucking traffic,' she exploded, tumbling into the hallway.

Behind her came Dorothy from Alice's consciousness-raising group. 'I'm terribly sorry I'm late. But they were out in force this evening. Couldn't put a pin between them on the Holloway Road. I had to go all round the houses. Ended up catching a cab at the corner.'

'Hey, Milly,' said Alice, 'guess what I said to my boss?'

Two men entered. One was huge, the other smaller, but broad. The huge one extended a hand. 'Bert Langley. Remember me from school? This is Greg.'

'Bert,' said Alice, 'You're enormous these days.'

'Late,' said Greg. 'Have we missed the main do?'

'Come on in,' said Alice.

In the living room she found the stragglers hadn't gone home after all. Sue and Lewis were still on the sofa, Dave Godwin, Lawrence and Rosemary were still arguing in the window alcove; Douglas had also reappeared, so had Richard Moresby, Trudi, Fiona, Miss Burrows, Gerald, Joey and several of the men from the bookbinding plant. They must all have been having a pee or fetching cigarettes from their coat pockets, or taking a look at the garden, the kitchen, the bedroom. She hoped they hadn't found anything untoward under the bed.

Bruno Barkworth and friends selected some music.

'Oh God,' said somebody who wasn't one of Bruno's friends, 'not Bryan Adams, pu-lease!'

Bruno and friends weren't listening. They were dancing in a circle as girls in a disco do; but wildly, arms beating the air, feet lifting from the floor and stomping down again, quite unlike girls.

Greg stepped into the room, stopped short, then made a bee-line for Fiona. He touched her elbow. 'Still got Snotty?' he asked softly.

'I beg your pardon,' said Elizabeth. She looked at the man. He seemed faintly familiar. A broad, foreign-looking man with gold rings on his fingers. He was, she supposed, of an age to have been one of her children; there had been so many children, she could hardly be sure.

'Elizabeth,' Fiona explained, 'this is my husband, Greg. He's talking about the teddy bear he won for me. At the Bank Holiday Fair on the Heath. We called it Snotty.'

'Fiona, I do have a regular job these days,' said Greg.

Someone who wasn't having a good time, it seemed to Alice, was reedy Richard. There he was, in a corner, unspeaking, staring. By his side stood a woman with dark, wiry hair, who looked Scottish.

Alice crossed the room 'You doing okay?' she asked. 'Want to introduce me?'

He turned his pale face to hers. He smiled, a thin, determined smile. He nodded.

'My wife, Jeannie. This gathering,' he waved, 'has confirmed what already, in my heart, I knew. It is in solitude,' he announced, 'that my Muse resides.'

'Fair enough,' said Alice.

'Soon,' he went on, 'I shall return to the ascetic regime of my bare-bricked cell. But this time,' he paused, 'I will take a dictionary.'

'Terrific,' said Alice. 'You must be the only person who's buying.'

'Hey.' Bruno grasped her arm. 'Why aren't you dancing?'

'I hadn't planned on it.'

Why shouldn't she, though? The formal bit was over, she loved dancing and she hadn't in ages. Besides they were playing Steve Winwood and her feet could hardly stay still; she longed to stretch, to twist, to romp, to flex her muscles. She joined the circle.

'I only go to parties for the dancing,' said Bruno.

Oh how good to move her body, to feel it working, to have it work, with pleasure, in response to the music. Almost as good as good sex. Alice could feel the music vibrating in her spine, *just* like good sex.

But Alice needed a sip of water. At the table she came across Milly Moxon and Dorothy hobnobbing over a bottle of gin.

'The thing is,' Dorothy was explaining, 'I'm terrified people will think I was drunk.'

'No harm in that. Look at Jeffrey Bernard.'

'Yes, but not in a bank. And not at my level. You can count the number of women branch managers on one hand. My colleagues are all on red alert for just one wrong move. You've no idea.'

'One of the High Streets, eh?' said Dave Godwin. 'How do you find you interface with the local council' The two women glared at him.

.

Bert touched Alice's arm. 'We're sorry we stole your word wall.'

She swallowed her Highland Spring. 'Water under the bridge. What are you doing these days?'

'On the door at the Nightmare. Only to pay the rent. See my name in lights any day now.' He drew a deep breath and expanded his chest. 'Stand-up comic,' he announced proudly.

'You ought to meet Lewis Black.' Alice put down her glass and steered him in the right direction. 'I'm sure he'd have you on *Celebrity Scrabble*.' Bert grinned from ear to ear.

Alice, on her own again, decided to change into trainers before she danced again, the black boots weren't as comfortable as they were elegant.

But in the hallway she discovered the party had turned torrential; people were pouring through the front door at an alarming rate. She hardly spotted a face she recognised. People in the hall moved to accommodate the newcomers, edging, so far as she could tell, into the already packed bedroom. Either the flat would burst at the seams or people's arms and legs would begin to stick out of the windows. What could she do?

She 'Excuse me'd' her way towards the kitchen. Through the open bathroom door she saw a row of people perched on the edge of the tub, chattering. In the kitchen she tried to suggest people might have more room to breathe on the patio, then discovered that was already full. Beyond, the dark lawn gave off a steady hum of conversation. She struggled back inside. Oh dear. More strangers were leaning against the hob, squeezing slivers of lime into the necks of bottles of Sol.

'Problems?' Bert's head appeared above the crowd. She explained.

'Ha! Gatecrashers. Leave it to me and Greg.'

'No rough stuff, please,' Alice begged his retreating back.

After that there seemed no let up in the number of new arrivals; though they *were* better dressed.

Alice struggled into the bedroom. How could she manage to unearth her trainers in this packed room? Who were all these people? Why had they shown up?

'Minute we sussed,' she heard a thickset man in a ribbed sweater tell his neighbour, 'where Lewis Black was headed, the word went out among the camera crews. Has a nose for the best bashes does Blackface.'

'I heard about it at the Nightmare Club,' said a very young woman with a mane of fair hair which reached well below the hem of her purple lycra mini. She smiled brightly. 'Isn't it wonderful how good news gets around?'

The man nodded. 'Do of the month looks like.'

'Oh no,' thought Alice, 'not a whole clubful! The Nightmare was huge. And camera crews! There must be dozens of them.' But she could hardly claim this was a private affair.

'You lost something?' the cameraman asked. 'My trainers.' 'Under the bed. Jack came across them while he was looking for his six-pack.'

When Alice regained the living room, she found it heaving with dancers; and Bruno's lot were still raving. She wriggled into their circle. One of the men had a long streaky wig which he dumped on one reveller's head after another. Occasionally the wig fell on the floor and lay there, like a dead cat, until someone else picked it up. This time it landed on Alice's head. 'Hey! Tina Turner!' they all shrieked. Alice danced over to the mantel and looked in the mirror. She rather liked the effect. Quite mad.

'Alice,' called Bert. 'Someone's unloading a whole heap of stuff outside. Looks like a drum kit and amps.'

Alice struggled her way to the front door again. It was open. 'Mike!' she cried.

Then she thought, why had he turned up? Why now? Was he — like Dave Godwin and Joey and Bert and Greg and the man from the bookbinding factory — impressed by her *City Limits* ad?

But, 'Brought the band.' Several thin men in tight black leather trooped past him carrying equipment. 'I'm into music promotion these days. This is Sandy, the vocalist! He waved towards a young black guy, also in leathers, but baggy ones; and a red baseball cap worn back to front. 'Saw the ad and thought this would be the ideal first gig. Low key,' he explained, then added, 'Purely for the experience. No charge to you.'

Should she tell him to come in? To go? But in the meantime it dawned on her, 'Mike, you're wearing a shell suit!'

'So?'

'It's bright pink. It doesn't go with your hair. People dress toddlers in them.'

'Well you're wearing trainers.'

Dave Godwin appeared. 'Trouble?' he asked, then, 'Alice, what on earth is that on your head?'

'A wig.'

'Up to her what she wears,' said Mike.

'Mike you'll spoil the look of the party,' said Alice. 'I'm supposed to be a bit of a celebrity right now. I can't, well, introduce someone who's wearing a shell suit. Couldn't you change? I'm sure you left some jeans behind.'

But, 'Have to help the band set up. I'll catch you in a bit,' he said and squeezed away through the crowd.

'Left some jeans behind where?' demanded Dave Godwin.

Alice slipped out of the front door. She stood in the garden, cooling off and watching the fun and games as though she were an outsider. Seeing Mike again was a bit much. Seeing him in a shell suit was something else.

Greg and Fiona danced cheek to cheek, just as they had in the early, idyllic days of their marriage. The music stopped and was replaced by a series of high pitched whines. Greg and Fiona stood close together in the circle of each other's arms.

'Here,' said Mike to Peter. 'Could you put some of these,' handing him a pile of dictionaries, 'on top of the amps? Help to diffuse the sound rather than have it all rise.'

'No waking up the neighbours, eh?' said Douglas.

'Some hope,' said Lawrence. But all three men pitched in and helped Mike and the band set up.

It was closing time at the pub on the corner. Everyone spilled out of the public bar and down the road and — attracted by the noise — onto Alice's front lawn. Several men lurching along the Holloway Road lurched off it and joined the throng.

Bert tapped Greg on the shoulder, 'Give us a moment, could you? Seem to be a load of winos at the door. Real undesirable elements.'

Which was how it happened that Alice was locked out. She rang the bell, then tried banging on the window, but now the live music had begun, she hadn't a hope in hell of being heard.

Never mind. After Bert and Greg's appearance the winos left. And she could just as well listen from out here. On second thoughts, given the noise the party was making, perhaps she'd better pop upstairs and to the neighbours on either side and see if they'd like to come and join in.

'Alice, where's Alice?' demanded Bert. 'Alice, it's the police, they want a word.'

No one seemed to have seen her.

'Oh good,' said Alice, returning with the neighbours, 'the door's open. I was afraid they wouldn't hear us.'

Two uniformed PCs stood in front of it. Where had she come across them before? She groped in her mind for the memory. Goodness, her past was rising up like bile.

'Are you the owner of these premises?' one of the PCs asked.

She nodded. 'Complaints from the neighbours. Keep the noise down, please.'

'They've withdrawn them,' said Alice. 'They're all here.'

In the hallway she ran across Mike still wearing the shell suit. 'Good band, aren't they?' he asked, then disappeared again.

Alice retreated to the table for another swig of Highland Spring, but couldn't find any and made do with white wine straight from the bottle. She looked up to find Sue's mother glaring at her. 'Just shows I was right,' she clearly heard her tell Timothy. 'I warned Susan about that girl. Disgraceful.' But although Alice could hear, she was sure that Sue, on the other side of the room with Lewis, couldn't. And if her mother enjoyed being right and it didn't hurt anyone, what the hell?

'All I really want,' Joey explained to Rosemary, 'is someone to care for, to protect . . . to worry about.' He paused, then added, 'Someone like you.'

'No one's ever wanted to protect me before,' said Rosemary, gazing up at him.

The photographer was having a whale of a time, snapping away at the band — and at all the celebrities. He just hoped he had enough film.

'What sort of shutter speed do you use in this light?' Alice heard Mike ask.

And Douglas? Alice'd hardly seen him all evening; but there he was, surrounded by cans of lager and talking to Gerald. What were they talking about? Douglas shifted one of the cans an inch or so. Gerald moved one of the others. Of course, they must be talking Second World War.

So they were happy too.

And Alice was happy — wasn't she? — because she was clean out of dictionaries. The strangers — impressed by her status as central celebrity of the evening — all bought copies. Alice had pocketed a small mint of money. Enough anyway to allow her to contemplate remaining self-employed. Added to whatever the sale of the carriage clock brought in.

5 a.m. The band had long since stopped playing, packed up their equipment and left. Michael Franks had been on the stereo, then Aretha Franklin, then Michael Bolton. Yearning, mournful, nostalgic music. Now there was silence apart from the turntable spinning round with a small, repeated hiss. Alice

was too tired to rise and switch it off. Was Alice, in fact, asleep?

She opened her eyes. People were lolling on the floor in couples, in small groups drinking coffee, examining empty bottles for overlooked dregs and discussing whether to go to a workman's café for bacon and eggs or up to Parliament Hill Fields to watch the sunrise.

She closed them. Was Mike still here? She'd hardly spoken to him all evening. He'd hardly spoken to her. Were they not speaking on account of the shell suit? Or for some other reason?

She opened them. Yes, he was still here; and Mike and Alice left the guests to it and . . .

She closed them. 5 a.m. The band had long since stopped playing and Mike came up to Alice as she sat on the floor among the becoming-early-morning debris, as she sat with her success strewn visibly around her. He was wearing jeans and he came up to her, bent over her, extended a hand. She took it, rose, followed him, still holding the hand which held hers, into the bedroom.

Mike and Alice left the guests to it and heaved the remaining coats off the duvet and . . .

Or. Alice was sitting with the soles of her trainers flat on the carpet, knees raised, the fabric of her culottes spread out in two triangles, like black bats, on either side of her thighs. Mike sat beside her, cross-legged. In this scenario, too, he wore jeans. Between his knees he held a wine bottle and a knife. He tapped the knife on the bottle, over and over. He stopped, then repeated the same snatch of rhythm. 'Cha-cha,' he explained to Alice. 'Listen.' He tapped again. 'Cha, cha, cha-cha-cha.'

'You hear it?' he asked. Alice nodded. He tapped again. He trawled the carpet with one hand and came up with a Budweiser can. He placed it between his knees and rapped on it with his finger nails. 'Much lighter sound,' he informed her. 'Tinny by comparison.' And returned to his efforts with the wine bottle and the knife.

Then, 'So you've been busy?' he asked.

'Busy?'

'By the look of this evening. Morning.' He stopped clattering and gave a small wave of his knife in the direction of the other people.

'I suppose.' He turned to her and held out his hand and pulled her to her feet and Alice saw the muscles in his arm tighten and the bones in his wrist stand out white under the skin and . . .

Or. Alice was sitting with the soles of her trainers flat on the floor etc . . . Mike was leaning against the living room door jamb, looking at people. He was wearing the shell suit. He looked at Alice and raised his eyebrows, the right one slightly higher than the left, a clichéd gesture, but effective nonetheless. He crossed the room and held out his hand and pulled her to her feet and Alice . . .

Or, better still, given the shell suit, Alice looked at him leaning against the door jamb, rose and crossed the room and he held out his hand and . . .

Or. Alice crossed the room and held out her hand and . . .

She opened her eyes. One way or another — whichever way it was — Alice and Mike left the guests to it and heaved the remaining coats off the duvet, dumped them in the hall and went to bed.

Alice kept her eyes open. She kept them open and watched Mike remove the shell suit — very swiftly, because it was elasticated at the waist, no zip, no buttons. And without the shell suit he looked as he had before, except for the red mark the elastic had left round his middle.

They started foreplay. 'I'm glad you're back,' said Alice.

'How d'you mean?'

'Back,' Alice repeated. 'Here.'

'I haven't been anywhere. Only around.'

'But around didn't include here?'

He shrugged. 'You know how it is. You wouldn't like to try this the other way round?'

'No,' said Alice.

'Why not?'

'Just not.'

'All right. Stick to what you were doing. A bit lower if you don't mind.'

'I think I do.'

'Why? Quarter of an inch at the most. Probably less.'

Alice sat up. 'I thought we had some kind of arrangement.'

He shook his head. 'You know I'm a loner. I mean this is fun. But nothing permanent. I could be off again any minute. So could you. Nothing to stop us.' He grinned as though including her in his plans.

Alice froze.

Like a stone.

Not like a stone, like something smaller and ever smaller, shrunken, shrivelled, like a prune, no like a withered head, a scalp, a dead, drained, bloodless, useless artefact: a worthless remnant of some ancient, alien culture which, these days, was an object of disgust. And as Alice thought this, 'Where are you?'

asked Mike, so she must have shrunk away physically. 'In your head, I mean. Don't you like this or what? We can do something else. We can do whatever you like.'

'Oh,' said Alice, still petrified, like a fossil, in an earlier age.

'I could tie you up,' Mike invited. 'You could tie me?'

She shook her head, slowly.

'How about stroking my balls? You like that.'

She shook her head again.

'What then?' He was looking at her, puzzled. 'I don't know if you don't say.'

Fair enough, thought Alice, yes that was fair enough. So, 'Mike, what do you want? From me?'

'I want you to enjoy yourself.'

And that was fair enough, too. Was it, in fact, enough? 'So you're not planning to move back in?'

'Not if all those friends of yours keep dropping by. No time for socialising.'

'They're not here every day. It was a party. Besides, you couldn't meet them wearing a shell suit.'

'See my point?'

She shook her head.

'What?' asked Mike, still waiting.

'Nothing. I'm thinking.'

'You want me to leave you to it?'

'Where would you go? It's the middle of the night.'

He nodded. 'Not your problem.'

Which yes, of course, it wasn't. Mike could look after himself. She could look after herself. She liked looking after herself, dammit. She toyed with the idea of telling him, 'I'm a loner, as well,' then decided it wouldn't ring true as when, in old films, the woman responded, 'And I love you too, darling.' She gave a small snort of a giggle.

'Something funny?' asked Mike.

'No. Yes. I was thinking about scalps. And fossils.'

'Ammonites or trilobites?'

'No particular sort. Fossils in general.'

'I used to collect them as a kid,' Mike said, 'and sell them. I could do that these days if I wasn't into the music full time. Might make a nice sideline.'

Alice giggled again.

'You all right now?' he asked. She nodded.

'So can we get on?'

They did. And as they did Alice reflected that it wasn't after all — never had been — Mike's closeness to her which attracted; it was the distance between them which intrigued.

Could the same be said of language? she wondered as he moved her hand a quarter of an inch, probably less. Was what remained unspoken or unwritten of equal importance to what was? And if so, should she ask the printers to double-space the next edition of her dictionary? Or introduce wider margins? Because more space between the lines or around the text was, unlike a blank page, an invitation to fill the gaps with annotations, to expand on the meanings of the words already there. And — arguably — the larger the space, the distance between, the more generous the invitation and the more there could be, potentially, to add.

Founded in 1986, Serpent's Tail publishes the innovative and the challenging.

If you would like to receive a catalogue of our current publications please write to:

FREEPOST
Serpent's Tail
4 Blackstock Mews
LONDON N4 2BR

(No stamp necessary if your letter is posted in the United Kingdom.)

Transmission
Atima Srivastava

'Set in the ultra-trendy world of film and TV, *Transmission* both satirizes and in many ways celebrates the incestuous café and cutting room area around London's Soho, meanwhile taking on board racism, AIDS, love, sex and feminism . . . yup, this is a right-on "designer novel". It's also bloody good . . . the first great novel of 1992.'   *Events Southwest*

'A compulsive look at straight, young non-drug users with HIV, inter-racial relationships and the ethics of working in TV.'   *The Face*

Absence Makes the Heart
Lynne Tillman

'In *Absence Makes the Heart* Lynne Tillman lures us onto unfamiliar ground with utterly persuasive, utterly duplicitous candor. Once there, we shall never be brought safely home. Her writing leaves our assumptions about life and art a shambles and, because it is funny and revealing, we relish it; but, reader, beware — you will be getting more than you either expect or deserve.' HARRY MATHEWS

'Lynne Tillman has the strongest, smartest, most subtly distinct writer's voice of my generation. I admire her breadth of observation, her syntax, her wit.' GARY INDIANA

'These bizarre short stories make alluring reading.'
Time Out

The South
Colm Tóibín

'*The South* is a daring, imaginative feat; the world it conjures is at once familiar and strange, and strangely moving. A splendid first novel.' JOHN BANVILLE

'Controlled and understated, this is a strong debut.' PATRICK GALE, *Gay Times*

'An imaginative, deeply felt and evocative tale.' *Sunday Times*

'A novel of clever, evocative observation . . . an intelligent, offbeat performance.' *Image*